Copyright © 2019 by Tom Reynolds

All rights reserved.

No part of this book may be reproduced in any form or by any electronic or mechanical means, including information storage and retrieval systems, without written permission from the author, except for the use of brief quotations in a book review.

OMNI'S FALL

TOM REYNOLDS

ONE

It's impossible to overstate how much I hate math class. I hate everything about it. Seriously, from the teacher, to the textbook, to the weirdly musty classroom we sit in every day of the week…

It stinks.

Literally.

Literally stinks.

And it's getting to me. My "academic work," or lack thereof, has become a problem for Michelle, so I've been spending a lot more time in this classroom than normal. Last week she came to reassure me their priority here is to ensure I receive a proper, real-world education on top of my extracurricular training.

The problem is my extracurricular activities have become more than extra.

Does that make them curricular activities then?

I'm not sure, and I forgot to ask.

I know she's worried because she doesn't want any flags raised. She's insisted I take two weeks off from training to concentrate on my studies. Ever since Midnight started helping Michelle bring up the training program's standards, his paranoia has been rubbing off on her. And that's the real reason why I'm sitting in this boring classroom, discreetly breathing through my mouth because of the horrible stench.

The academy had opened the school in a hurry and must not have cleaned these old gross velvet drapes that have been sitting here for a decade.

"And what is x for this equation, Mr. Connolly?" Mr. Muldowney asks.

Uh-oh. I haven't been paying attention. Better come up with something fast.

"Hmm, hard to say."

"If you had to take a wild guess."

"2?"

There's laughter from the rest of the class. I hear someone whisper the word *dummy* under their breath.

"14.7."

"I was close."

"You were not close, Mr. Connolly. Stop daydreaming and start paying more attention to what's going on up here. We can discuss this further after class."

Great. This entire time I was counting down the seconds until I could leave this musty old dungeon, and now I have even more time tacked on.

This is Mr. Muldowney's class, and I'm not exaggerating when I say it's torture. Math has never been my strong suit. Transferring schools and then missing numerous classes this semester hasn't helped.

But by far it's Mr. Muldowney who takes the class from irritating to torturous. He's had it out for me since day one. He's never said as much, but I can tell. It's all in the way he talks. He uses a different tone with me than with every other student. He doesn't think I belong in this class or this school, and he doesn't hide it.

The worst part is that everyone else loves him. He's one of the "cool teachers," which lets him get away with picking on me, a kid at the academy who doesn't really *belong* here. I'm only here because a couple of metahumans destroyed my school.

Okay, so one of those metahumans was me, but I didn't *mean* to destroy my school. Even I'm not stupid enough to believe destroying my school would suddenly mean I wouldn't have to go anymore. Instead, I was sent here, where I hardly know anyone and people like Mr. Muldowney seem hell-bent on constantly reminding me I'm an outsider.

He's back at the whiteboard, showing how he solved for x and then moving on to the next equation. My phone vibrates in my pocket.

The academy lets us keep our phones with us due to the recent rise in metahuman activity and the need to keep us in contact in case of an emergency. Pulling your phone out during class, however, is a quick way to get it put in a drawer for the rest of the period.

It buzzes again. A series of long buzzes followed by short ones.

The long buzzes tell me it's a breaking news alert. The short ones tell me that the event is active and could use metahuman attention.

The buzzes follow a series of rules and triggers that Jim put together to keep me connected to the outside world, even while I'm stuck in class. The idea is for me to relax and rest assured that the world is still spinning without my having to constantly check my phone for trouble.

It's worked out well so far, since Jim set the threshold

for notifications pretty high. It's only supposed to go off in cases of an extreme global emergency, although one time it went off because Jim's favorite energy drink was on sale. Apparently he copied over the same rules he'd applied to his phone to mine.

I inch my right hand over to my pocket and slip it inside. The phone is still vibrating with the same series of long and short buzzes, signaling this is a real emergency.

Mr. Muldowney has his back to me, drawing out a never-ending equation on the whiteboard, so I quickly take my phone out and scan the screen.

BREAKING: Meltdown Imminent at Asana Nuclear Power Plant

That can't be good.

I glance up to check on Mr. Muldowney just as he turns to face the class. His eyes catch mine, and I adjust my posture, dropping my phone into my lap and placing both hands on my desk as naturally as possible.

His eyes narrow with suspicion, but he doesn't stop the lesson.

He faces the whiteboard again, and I steal another glance down at my phone. There's a notification on the display. It looks like it's from a free-to-play game where they try to get you to buy more gems or crystals or whatever if you don't want to wait to play, but it's not.

It's a custom-designed app from Michelle's team. Every metahuman embedded at the school has it since she can't exactly send us a text message saying, *Metahumans, we need help!*

The notification says there's a special free crystal event taking place, and I have to swipe the alert to join. I casually swipe at the display. After bio-authenticating myself, the phone opens the app. The cartoon Viking loading screen disappears, and I'm greeted with a map of the Pacific region, with a bull's-eye on the location of the meltdown.

At the bottom of the screen is a list of other metahumans at the school. Most names are grayed out, meaning they haven't received the notification yet. Others are in a bright red font, showing who's unavailable. Only a couple are highlighted in green, indicating they've received the call and are on their way.

My name, or rather my alter ego's name, Omni, is highlighted in red. This isn't because I've chosen to take myself out of the fight, but because Michelle knows I'm in class, and according to her, that means I'm unavailable. She says I've missed too much time as it is, and she can't keep providing excuses for me to skip out on class.

I understand, in theory, but as I'm looking at the list of metahumans responding to the call, I'm not feeling particularly confident. Some of the responders are relatively low on the overall metahuman power scale. Not that their powers aren't useful, but mind control and invisibility won't do much to stop a nuclear reactor from melting down.

Mr. Muldowney is still at the board, so I take a chance and send a message:

These guys won't be enough. Do you need me?

The reply comes almost instantly:

Absolutely not. If you miss Muldowney's class again, you're facing suspension. Other metahumans from around the world are en route. We'll handle it. Stay in class.

"Is there something about your lap that's more interesting than what is happening up here, Mr. Connolly?"

Crap. Muldowney is standing mere feet from me. Guess my senses aren't very super without my metabands turned on. The app detects that my attention has been diverted and automatically closes to keep anyone from seeing the interface and asking questions.

"No, there's not, Mr. Muldowney. Sorry," I reply.

"Surely there must be. You were staring at your lap for quite some time."

I try to think fast, hoping he stays put so he won't notice the phone in my lap.

"No, I was just nodding off."

The class reacts with a mixture of *ohhhs* and laughter.

"Not that your class is boring or anything," I backpedal. "It's not. I didn't get a lot of sleep last night, that's all."

"You are on extremely thin ice, Mr. Connolly."

Whew, he didn't notice the phone.

It's 1:42. Three minutes until I'm out of here anyway. Probably should have just waited out the clock.

Outside the classroom windows, there are growing storm clouds. As I'm looking, there's a loud sonic boom and a blue blur streaks across the sky.

The entire class jumps out of their seats and rushes to the windows to see what the sound was. Many are used to seeing metahumans now, but it's rare to see one so close to the school. The other students from my old school are no doubt having flashbacks to when a metahuman tore our school apart. It's hard to let those negative associations go.

"All right, everyone. All right. Let's all have a seat," Mr. Muldowney says, now holding his tablet. "It says here there is a nuclear reactor malfunction underway in Southeast Asia. That's likely where that metahuman is heading. No need to worry about something happening seven thousand miles away."

Seven thousand miles? That's a long way, even when you can fly and have super speed. Now I wish I'd paid more attention during math so I could calculate how long it'd take me to fly there.

If the reactor is close to critical, then every second counts.

"Mr. Muldowney, can I be excused?" I say, raising my hand even though it doesn't matter.

"Excuse me, Mr. Connolly? You haven't been paying attention the entire class, and now you want to leave early?"

"It's an emergency."

"Oh, I suppose you have to go help out in Asia?"

The other students laugh.

I do actually, smartass, but I can't say that.

"No, a different kind of emergency, I swear," I say.

"You'll have to tell me what the emergency is, I'm afraid."

"It's a... bathroom kind."

This earns me an even bigger round of laughter.

"There are two minutes left in class, Mr. Connolly. I'm sure you can hold it."

Outside, there's another sonic boom as a metahuman flies past, heading in the same direction as the last one.

"I can't," I blurt out.

My palms are starting to sweat. Why are so many metahumans responding? It must be bad.

"You can't wait two more minutes? How on earth is that possible?"

Do or die time.

If I wanted out of this class right now, I'd have to swallow my pride and pull deep.

"Diarrhea," I say, barely above a whisper.

"I'm sorry, I didn't catch that," Mr. Muldowney says.

He definitely caught it, but even he can't believe I'm embarrassing myself like this.

"I have diarrhea," I say loudly so he won't ask a third time.

The entire classroom erupts into fits of laughter. Even Mr. Muldowney can't suppress a smirk.

"Wow, okay, Mr. Connolly. If it is truly that terrible, you may go use the facilities."

Before he even finishes his sentence, I discretely pocket my phone and jump out of my chair, heading for the door. The class laughs even harder at my urgent exit. I blow right past the bathroom pass hanging from a peg by the door. I won't need it.

Everyone always assumes that being a metahuman is glamorous work. No one ever tells you, sometimes you have to pretend you're about to crap your pants.

TWO

Once I'm in the hallway, I take in a deep breath of fresh air, and then it's time to find a place to activate my metabands. Activating them on school grounds is a huge no-no in Michelle's book, but I don't have many other options. Outside is better than inside, though.

"Hey, you," someone behind me shouts as I hurry down the hallway.

I glance back at the student hall monitor hurrying toward me. She looks mad, and I don't have time for this. I ignore her and continue walking.

"I'm talking to you!"

I pick up my pace. Behind me, I hear her do the same. Then her footsteps switch from a walk to a jog. Looks like she's giving me no choice.

I take off running, blowing my pursuer's jogging pace right out of the water. Her footsteps quicken to try and match mine. She hurls another shout my way, but there's no way she, or anyone else, will stop me now. I hope she didn't recognize me.

Since the security procedure to get on campus is strict,

the school buildings are more lax. I take a left and find a door leading outside. I push it and it easily pops open. Outside, I quickly close the door and lean up against it until I hear the hall monitor run past.

There's a sports equipment shed nearby. It's not the perfect place to activate, but it'll have to do. There's no way I can access the Blair Building or any of the underground facilities without alerting Michelle, and that's if she'd even let me enter.

The bell rings, releasing the rest of the students from class. I don't have long now.

As I jog toward the equipment shed, I pull my phone out of my pocket. If I'm going to fly to Asia, it'd be a good idea to figure out the general direction I should go in first.

A message pops up on my screen from Jim. It's brief.

Are you on this?

I take the wireless earbud out of my other pocket, pop it into my ear, then tap on Jim's name to connect with him.

"Where are you?" he asks as soon as the comms device establishes the connection. No time for small talk.

"I'm heading to the storage shed near the lacrosse field."

"How did you get outside already? The bell just rang."

In the background, I can hear lockers slamming and people talking.

"I got out a few minutes early," I say.

"Oh, Michelle won't be happy about that."

"That's why I've got you, Jim. You wouldn't happen to know the quickest way to Asia, would you?"

"Are you serious?"

"Yeah, I'm serious. I know it's on the other side of the world, but should I head west or east? Or is it the same either way?"

Behind me, the door I exited through slams open. I tell

myself it's just the other students leaving, but I don't venture a glance back. I quicken my pace, trying not to look like I'm running away from anything.

"Man, I don't know," Jim whines.

"That's him," the hall monitor shouts.

"Mr. Connolly?" Mr. Muldowney calls out.

That stupid hall monitor must have ratted me out. Still, there's no need to panic. I'm not Mr. Connolly, so there's no reason to turn around and respond. That's what someone who isn't Mr. Connolly would do in this situation.

"Mr. Connolly. I know it's you."

No, he doesn't. Not for sure, at least.

Now I'm almost running. If I don't turn around and acknowledge him, he'll never be 100% sure it was me. That seems logical, right?

I make my way past the tennis courts and turn right, increasing the distance between myself and the main campus buildings.

"Uh ... west," Jim says through the earpiece.

"Are you sure?"

"Like 99% sure. It's hard to get accurate directions when you can't tell any of these apps you can fly."

"Sounds like a million-dollar idea, Jim. Just think of all the metahumans who could benefit from an app like that."

I reach the storage shed and turn the corner just as footsteps approach from behind me. The door is propped open, and I slip inside and close the door behind me. Just to be safe, I drag a nearby box in front of the door to keep it securely closed. The shed smells stale with sweat, but I don't plan on staying here long.

I flick my arms out to my sides, and the metabands appear around my wrists. It takes less concentration than ever to materialize them now. I strike them together to activate, and Omni's dark red suit flows out from the bracelets to engulf my body. Just as the transformation is completed, the shed door rattles.

I'd bet dollars to donuts that it's Mr. Muldowney trying to open the door, even though I've never really been sure what that phrase means.

"Open this door right now," Mr. Muldowney orders.

Well, I won my bet with myself.

"Quick hypothetical question, Jim. Any idea how I can get out of the sports storage shed near the lacrosse fields without Muldowney seeing me?" I whisper.

"Mr. Muldowney is there?" he asks in surprise.

"He kinda, sorta, maybe followed me out of his classroom, and now I'm trapped inside the shed with him outside."

"Not smart, Connor. If your metabands were fully functional, you could teleport out of there."

Teleportation is one power that has eluded me since my fight with the Alphas. Inaccurate teleportation would work in this situation, but I can't even do that. When I try to teleport, the ability just isn't there anymore. A consequence of my cracked and damaged metabands.

The jostling at the door has turned into banging. I remain as still and quiet as possible. I'm the only one who can give me away right now.

"Any chance you could create a distraction for me, Jim?"

"A distraction? Are we talking about the same Muldowney? That guy is many things, but easily distracted isn't one. I'm across campus, anyway."

"How long would it take you to get here?"

"Umm, like fifteen minutes. Not all of us have super speed, remember?"

"Super speed. Great idea, Jim."

"You might want to think about using it. According to news reports, that reactor is almost critical. If you want to help, you'll have to get there soon."

With no room to maneuver in the shed, getting up to speed will be difficult. Still, it's my only way out of here without anyone seeing me or blowing a hole through the roof, something that would undoubtedly lead to a very livid Michelle.

I wait for the right moment, focusing my attention on the door. By shifting the wavelength of my vision, I can see Mr. Muldowney waiting beyond the solid aluminum door.

"Come on, get out of the way," I mumble to myself.

He's on his phone directly in front of the door, no doubt calling security to come and open the shed. If he'd just step to his right...

"Jim, I need you to call Muldowney's cell phone," I whisper.

"What? Are you crazy?"

"I know you have the faculty contact list. Bring up Muldowney's phone number and call him."

"And say what?"

"I don't care. Just get him away from this door."

"But—"

"I don't have time for buts, Jim. If I don't get out of this shed soon, I'll have to power down so Muldowney doesn't find Omni sitting on a pile of lacrosse nets."

"Fine."

I hear Jim dial the number after he's muted my side of the call. Muldowney picks up the call on the first ring.

"Um, is this Muldowney?" Jim asks.

"This is *Mr.* Muldowney. Who am I speaking to?"

Jim responds with a series of ums and uhs as he tries to think of a clever response.

He fails.

"Who am I? I'm, um, the police."

"The police?" Mr. Muldowney asks.

"Yes, that's me. I'm the police. I'm a police officer, is what I meant to say. I've got some bad news. It's your car. We had to tow your car."

Tow your car? That's the best Jim could come up with?

"Why on earth did you tow my car? I parked it in the faculty lot with a faculty sticker on the windshield. This is outrageous!"

Irritated, Mr. Muldowney steps away from the shed and stands on his tiptoes to peer across the lacrosse field at the faculty parking lot a hundred yards away.

Now is my chance.

Crouched down in the dark, time slows around me as I take my first step toward the door. Behind me, the dust is just starting to kick up into the air. I slide the box keeping the door shut out of the way. I can usually move at superhuman speed without causing much disturbance, as long as I'm moving fast enough, but the door is unavoidably in my way.

I slowly push it open to avoid drawing attention, but as I push, I glimpse Muldowney slowly turning toward me. His reflexes are quicker than I expected. If I keep opening the door at this speed, I'll still be here when he fully turns, and I can't have that.

Oh well.

Time compresses further, and everything around me looks frozen in place. Relative to how fast I'm moving, it basically is.

I push the door all the way open, careful not to break

the sound barrier. A sonic boom would undermine my attempt at staying undercover.

What I can't prevent is the mass of displaced air I've sent speeding in Muldowney's direction, caused by the door's rapid movement. The air is moving almost as fast as I am, and I watch as it collides with Muldowney, knocking him off his feet. His expression remains frozen, and he's still holding his phone up to his ear. He'll have no idea who or what knocked him over, but at least he won't be hurt.

Now with Muldowney out of the way, it's time for me to head for Asana.

THREE

I'm running so fast Muldowney and the academy are miles behind me in an instant. I gain speed as I run across empty fields and over mountains. There's a city up ahead, and I consider running around it, but the detour would cost me too much time, so I plow straight through instead. I'm weaving in and out of traffic and crowds as the world stands still around me.

Outside the city, the coastline stretches up ahead. I'm close to my top speed when my feet hit the sand and I leap into the air.

The momentum launches me over the ocean, and time returns to normal as the shore disappears behind me.

"Are you okay, sir?" Jim asks through my earpiece.

"I'm out and I'm fine. Gotta admit, I could get used to you calling me 'sir,' Jim. Rolls off the tongue nicely," I reply.

"No, I'm not okay. I don't know what the hell happened, but a huge gust of wind just knocked me to the ground!"

Oh. Jim's still on the phone with Muldowney.

"Hang up that call, Jim," I tell him.

"If I hang up, he'll suspect I'm not really the police."

"He'll suspect that once he finds his car right where he left it this morning anyway."

"Good point."

There's a click on the other end of the line as Jim drops his call with Muldowney.

"Where am I heading?" I ask.

"Umm, turn left about… six degrees."

"Roger that."

With help from Midnight, we rigged my phone to work normally with my metabands active. Jim can access my coordinates and send anything he wants through the same custom app we're talking through. It's not always perfect, but it beats having to switch out my SIM card every time I cross a border.

"You're getting close. Time to ease off the gas."

Even though I can't fly as fast as I can run, I'm still going fast when Japan's coast takes shape on the horizon.

"I see it, Jim."

Up ahead, a large plume of white smoke is hanging high in the air. Below is a large facility close to the shore. This must be it.

I descend feet first. I find it puts people at ease, like I'm landing after taking a big jump instead of flying at them fist first like a homing missile.

On the ground, people the size of ants are scattering. A few are using a heavy-pressure fire hose to spray down the building. Mixed among them are a dozen metahumans carrying victims away from the scene. A man in a white hardhat is yelling and waving his arms at me.

I land beside him and say, "My name is Omni. I'm here to help."

"It's too late for help. We need to get everyone out of here!"

Between people running for safety and the dozens of pops and small explosions coming from inside the facility, the scene is chaotic, but I've lucked upon someone who speaks English.

Another metahuman lands beside me. She's dressed all in black, her face left unmasked.

"Darkweaver. Are you in charge?" she asks.

"Omni. No, I just got here."

"You know more than me, then. What can I do to help?"

"We need to get everyone out of here as fast as possible."

"Got it."

Without hesitation, Darkweaver closes her eyes and manifests a bubble, fifty feet in diameter and with a person-sized opening near the base.

"Get in, everyone! I'll take you to safety!"

But no one answers her call.

"The crews are trying to salvage the area by containing the fallout," the man in the hardhat explains. "If they fail, there's no telling how far the radiation will spread. You won't find anyone willing to run. I've been trying to evacuate them, but it's no use. They'll stay until the end to contain the disaster."

I stand beside the man and stare at the building. Aside from several fires, the building looks normal. It isn't glowing radioactive green or crumbling to the ground.

"How can we stop the meltdown from going critical?"

"You can't. The chain reaction is too far along. All we can hope for is to contain the damage and evacuate as many civilians as possible."

"There has to be something we can do."

"There's not. Everyone here is doing the only thing they can do."

Without another word, the man heads back toward the doomed facility. I stand in disbelief, trying to think of something, anything, I can do to stop this. There has to be something we can do. There's always something.

Through my earpiece Jim says, "Omni, are you—"

It cuts out.

"—think the radiation is—problems with the sig—"

Unable to withstand the radiation, the line goes dead.

"Get back! Everyone, get back!" a man in a HAZMAT suit yells as he runs from the building. "The reactor is going critical!"

On the outside, nothing about the building has changed, but everyone is taking his call to action seriously. Dozens of workers run past me. Their movements are clumsy and slow inside their containment suits. One person trips in front of me. I'm rushing to help him onto his feet when an idea hits me.

"Where's the core?" I ask him.

"It's in the building's center, in the subbasement. It doesn't matter now, though." He's running away again as he says, "We're too late."

Even the other metahumans are clearing out. In a matter of minutes, I'm the last person standing close to the facility. I glance down at my metabands, looking for any sign of trouble. They've sustained permanent damage, something previously thought impossible. I don't know if I'm immune to radiation, but based on how I feel, the metabands seem to be holding up.

Concentrating on my vision, I peel back the facility's layers. Near the building's center, I hit lead-lined walls, where my enhanced vision fails. All I can see is what looks like static combined with the kind of sunburst image you see after looking at the sun for too long.

This must be the core. In the seconds I've been looking at it, it's grown noticeably brighter.

I glance back at the people scurrying away. Some have stopped, too tired from the added weight of their suits. Others look as though they've given up. There just isn't enough time for them to escape the fallout radius.

I look back at the facility and the glowing center, visible only to me. If I'm going to do this, I'll have to be quick.

"Get out of there!" someone yells behind me.

I ignore him and hurl myself forward.

The world slows down again as I move faster and faster. I run through the first wall of the facility in an explosion of drywall and girders.

The next wall is stronger, concrete, but not enough to slow me down due to the speed I'm traveling.

The one after is lead-lined and tougher. I still burst through it, but it slows me down considerably.

The next is further reinforced. I can't plow through it at super speed and have to punch my way through instead.

I'm starting to feel funny. Not necessarily bad, just funny. Pins and needles shoot through my hands like they've fallen asleep. It's the radiation. I must be close to the core if I can literally feel it.

I try to use my heat vision to burn through the final lead wall, but it doesn't work. Whether it's my damaged metabands or the radiation permeating the air is something I'll have to figure out later.

Digging down deep, I focus my heat vision on a weak spot in the lead. I continue to focus my blast as I step back to build momentum. Then I take another running start at the wall.

I lead with my shoulder and punch a hole big enough to tear open with my hands.

Inside, everything is dark. There's a large deep pool of water that is boiling over.

Taking a deep breath, I plunge into the pool. The radiation overwhelms not just my sight, but my hearing too. There are constant near-deafening pops and hisses.

At the bottom of the pool, I find an elaborate rig holding together a series of metal rods throwing off an incredible amount of heat and energy.

I grab onto two handle-like protrusions, likely designed for robotic arms to attach to, not two human hands. The radiation is overwhelming, and my entire body feels numb, which might not be such a bad thing for the next part.

I assume the ceiling is reinforced with the same materials as the walls, but it's the quickest way out.

Readjusting my grip, I crouch down in the pool of radioactive water. Normally, when I fly, I look at where I'm going to avoid slamming into something. That's not a concern now.

This time, I tuck my chin against my chest, hoping my shoulders will take the brunt of the impact. But there isn't time to second guess myself. I push off against the bottom of the pool as hard as I can.

I rise so fast I don't notice the transition between water and air. All I feel is the first impact. Between the force and the radiation, my mind fails and dizziness hits me. But I have to keep going.

I fly higher and hit another ceiling. Without my previous momentum, I can't burst through it. I push with my shoulders, straining against the combination of lead and steel until a small hole develops in the dented ceiling. I push again, and the hole widens enough to let me through.

The next few ceilings are easier to break through, and I pick up speed as I pop through ceiling after ceiling and finally reach open air. The sky is clear and blue—a beautiful day belied by the horror below.

Making it out of the facility with the radioactive core intact was just the beginning. Now I need to get it clear of any populated areas, so I continue my trajectory. Without any physical obstacles to slow me, I quickly gain speed.

I consider flying the core out into the ocean, but unsure what effects that could have, I fly higher and higher. The only safe place to dispose of this is outer space, and I'd be deluding myself to think otherwise.

That's when it happens.

A blinding light, and an explosion.

The entire world goes white, and static fills my ears.

It takes me a few seconds to realize I'm not flying anymore.

Or holding anything in my arms.

I'm in free fall.

I hit the ground, and the impact is tremendous. The crater my body creates kicks earth and debris high into the air.

I lie still on the ground, trying to regain my bearings. The dizziness slowly fades. I hear yelling and footsteps. A pair of hands grabs me by the shoulders and drags me up and onto my feet.

"What the hell did you do?"

Dust and debris obscure my vision, but the emblem on his chest, the broad outline of an eagle in flight, gives him away.

His moniker is "Maverick," but he's anything but.

After popping up a few months ago, Maverick made a name and place for himself by leading a group of US government-sanctioned metahuman first responders. For the sake of plausible deniability in case anything ever went wrong, no government agency has confirmed having ties with the group, although with someone like Maverick, that wasn't a concern.

Maverick is little more than a walking public relations campaign. And I'm not just parroting what everyone else says about him online. I'm speaking from experience. I've responded to several emergencies around the globe where Maverick showed up after the hard part was over.

He's always late to the fight or rescue, but not out of laziness or poor timing. He's late so he won't have to get involved. Being a public metahuman who considers themselves a hero is risky. Sometimes you have to make hard choices when you have no other options.

So I'm not surprised he showed up at the site of a possible disaster late.

"Answer me!" he shouts, but I've already forgotten the question, and it's hard to hear over the sirens and airhorns.

"What happened? Is everyone safe?" I ask, though I'm terrified of what his answer might be.

I didn't think a nuclear core could explode, at least not like a bomb.

Maverick grabs me by the collar, and we're suddenly shooting up into the sky. We break through the smoke still pouring out of the power plant. Heat warms my back from the sun beating down on the landscape below.

"Why did you do that?" Maverick asks.

"I needed to get the core away from everyone. I needed to remove the danger. What happened? Was there a nuclear explosion?"

"No, but there was an explosion. The change in temperature, along with the rapid change in elevation, rapidly increased the instability of the core."

I remain silent, dreading his next words.

"It wasn't the same as a nuclear explosion. That can't happen by accident or with the type of nuclear fuel used here. But what you did was almost as bad. Do you know why they bury nuclear material so deep inside the reactor?"

I don't answer.

"It's meant to contain the damage and fallout of a meltdown. Sure, that doesn't help the workers much, but it does prevent the fallout from spreading. You screwed all that up."

"What do you mean? What's happening? We should be down there helping them."

I turn to fly back down to the scene of the accident, unsure if my metabands have enough juice left to do more than slow down my fall, but Maverick grabs my shoulders and stops me.

"There's nothing you can do now. There's nothing anyone can do. You may have saved lives today, but you also increased the area of exposure by hundreds of miles. The fallout is scattered now, and the area needs to be cleared out."

"Nobody died, then? That's good. They can come back."

"No, they can't. No human being will be allowed to set foot in this area for years, if not decades. People will have to pack up and abandon their entire lives now. You've destroyed countless businesses, families, and lives. Most of them will never have the chance to come back here again."

FOUR

The flight back home is taking ten times longer than the flight out. It's still the quickest way to travel, at least since I lost the ability to teleport, but it's taking me longer because of the state of my metabands.

After Jim made sure I was all right, I cut the comms link between us. I don't want him sharing any of the blame. Coming to Asana to save people from the reactor was my decision, after all.

I fly low over the Pacific Ocean. I don't have the strength or willpower to fly at high altitude, and I'm in no hurry, anyway. Below me, the ocean stretches into infinity in all directions. A pod of a dozen dolphins are swimming beneath me. Even though I'm still a hundred feet above the surface, they seem to sense my presence and match my speed.

In the distance, another metahuman is heading toward me. I worry she's coming to confront me, but she speeds past without slowing down.

I might be imagining things, but I swear she shook her head as she passed by.

Ahead, the coastline of the United States is approaching rapidly. Water turns to land below me and I turn north and retract part of my suit to fish my phone out of my pocket. There's a voicemail from Michelle waiting.

"Connor, I need to speak with you immediately. You know where to find me."

The voicemail ends abruptly. She's no doubt received a report on what went down in Asia, and there's no way she's happy about it. I can't blame her; I'm not happy about it either. I've disappointed myself, and there's little anyone can say or do to make me feel any better or worse.

I fly high over the academy, surveilling the area for onlookers. I don't want to end up in a shed again.

Like most things, powering down without being noticed used to be much easier when I could teleport. Now I have to scout the area before I land.

School is out for the day, making things easier on one hand, but harder on the other. It's still early enough for after-school practices to be underway. I'm a safe distance from the various practice fields, but I've always gotta keep an eye out for the damn cross-country team. They love running back here in these woods and going off trail, even though they're not supposed to.

I squint and shift my vision into the infrared spectrum to look through the tree cover. A few miles away, I spot a line of bodies running through the woods and decide it's safe to land here.

I rapidly descend through the tree canopy, avoiding branches as best I can. Once my feet are back on solid ground, I bring my metabands together and deactivate them. The crimson red suit retracts into the metabands, and I'm back to regular old Connor Connolly. If anyone happened upon me now, they'd just wonder why I was wandering around the woods by myself. Concentrating, I shift the metabands out of sync with our reality, vanishing them until they're needed again.

It's a short walk to the Blair Building, where Michelle is waiting for me deep underground. I'm still moving slowly to delay the inevitable, but it's useless. It won't make facing her any easier. Better to just rip the bandage off.

Inside the Blair Building I find the elevator that doubles as a classroom and ride it down to the training facility. Though the descent is always slow to keep it from attracting any unwanted attention, it feels especially long today.

The room reaches the bottom of the elevator shaft, and I exit into a long and quiet hallway. Several metahumans who used to train here have dropped out of school. When being a super-powered individual and a high school student at an exclusive preparatory academy becomes too hard to balance, the superhero side always wins. They might never be as good as they could have been had they finished the program, but after the first wave of metabands randomly stopped working a decade ago, many took to the opinion the same could happen to their metabands anytime. And if that were to happen, doesn't it make the most sense to use them as much as possible now?

Others had left for different reasons. They're the ones I spend a lot of time trying not to think about, like Ellie and Winston. In the fight against Alpha Team, they'd helped me put Charlie down once and for all by transferring the energy from their metabands into mine. What no one had realized was the power transfer would be permanent.

We'd all assumed that since metabands recharge themselves while powered down, theirs would also naturally recharge after the power was transferred into another set. That didn't happen. I'd effectively stripped them of their powers. Neither of them had ever blamed me, but I still feel tremendous guilt about it.

Midnight isn't even sure how it happened. According to him, their metabands should have recharged to optimal levels. His best guess is the extreme trauma I endured during the final clash, combined with the unique way my metabands were damaged, caused an unforeseen issue and now there are two fewer metahumans in the world.

I reach the end of the hallway and lift my hand to knock on the door to Michelle's office. Before my knuckles can reach the metal surface, Michelle tells me to come in. I turn the doorknob and find it unlocked.

Inside the office, Michelle has her back to me. She's seated at her desk, focused on a flurry of information streaming across her monitor. Her phone is caught between her ear and shoulder. I'm not sure who's on the other end, but I've never heard Michelle so stressed before.

"No, I understand… completely… yes, of course…"

I stand in the doorway, waiting for her to finish the call. She swivels her chair around to face me and gestures for me to take the seat in front of her desk.

"Understood. Thank you, sir," she says into the phone and hangs up. "You don't even want to know who that was," Michelle tells me.

Michelle has always been a serious person, but I've never seen her this serious before. She looks stressed out and tired. The normally neat documents on her desk look disorganized, like they've been rifled through.

"I want to hear your version of what happened today," she says.

"I screwed up."

"In your own words, please."

"I wasn't thinking. Or I was thinking, but I was thinking about the wrong thing, I guess. I didn't want anyone to get hurt, and I thought getting the core out of there was the best solution. The people there, they were selfless. They were willing to sacrifice themselves to stop the fallout from spreading, but I couldn't stand by and let them die. I had to try something."

"Did anyone tell you that removing the core from the cooling tanks would cause it to explode?"

"No, but I didn't ask either."

"Hmm." Michelle sat in thought for a moment. "Connor, do you know why I do what I do?"

I'd never really thought about it.

"You want to help?"

"That's a big part of it, but if I just wanted to *help,* there are other lines of work I could have gone into that would cause me less trouble. I chose to work with young metahumans because I think you all have the potential to create positive change. Maybe it's naive, but it's an idea I cling to when things get tough. Everyone makes mistakes, but not everyone makes them with the best interests of others at heart."

"Thanks?"

"That was the nice part. You violated several of the academy's rules. You left class early to engage in a mission you were not a part of. While many lives were saved today, you also caused untold damage, the full extent of which we may not know for decades.

"I want you at this school, Connor. I think it's beneficial for you, and I've gone through a lot of trouble not only to get you here, but to keep you here as well. That's why I'm afraid I must suspend your on-campus metaband use for the rest of the semester. You can use them down here in the facility while training, but you cannot activate them on campus for any reason until next semester."

"What? But what if I need them? What if the campus is under attack or there's an emergency?"

"Then we'll have to rely on other metas to take care of it. The reason behind not using your metabands on campus is to avoid drawing attention to the academy. There are people and organizations out there that would love to harm us. Our best defense against them is to make sure they never know we exist. Again, Connor, this is sacrificing something in the immediate to protect the future and others.

"I won't be confiscating your metabands today. I know how tied to them metas become after they're activated the first time and the longer they're worn. There's a bond between metabands and their users, and that's not something I want to interfere with. I want to trust you. However, if you choose to break the rules, you will force my hand. Do you understand?"

"Yeah."

"I'm serious, Connor. I'm already hearing rumblings there should be formal charges against you over the events in Japan. In the days and weeks to come, politicians and other metahumans will be coming out of the woodwork, demanding you be brought to justice and have your metabands confiscated for good. I will do everything in my power to prevent that from happening, I promise you, but I need you to follow my rules in return. I can't help you if you're not willing to let me."

"I understand, Michelle. I won't use them on campus again."

I'm suddenly overwhelmed with strange emotions. The idea that anyone could take my metabands has never crossed my mind. I hate that I've disappointed Michelle, but

I'm also touched that she cares so much about me. I feel like an idiot for never considering her before or how much she's risked for me without so much as a thank you.

"Okay. We'll discuss this again, but for now, I'm glad we're on the same page for a change. Since your classes are finished, for the day anyway—ahem, there's something else for you."

"Sure, what is it?"

"Midnight would like to speak with you."

Gulp.

"Don't worry," Michelle says, "it's not about your actions today. I've already spoken with him about it, and let's just say he and I don't necessarily share the same point of view."

That shouldn't come as a surprise. Midnight isn't one to justify sacrificing a life under any circumstances, nor is he one to care about the rules. He especially wouldn't care what other metahumans think about what I did today since he's never cared about what they think of his actions.

"Just remember what I said, Connor. No metabands on campus. You keep your word, and I'll protect you however I can."

FIVE

I ride the classroom elevator up to the real world and exit into the hallway of the Blair Building. It's quiet, as always, and this is the first time I'm alone with my thoughts without having to worry about flying over the Pacific Ocean.

I bring up the news on my phone, curious what the latest developments are. I check Derrick's site first, and I'm not surprised to find little mention of Omni specifically. Their coverage is mainly of the accident itself.

Other sites aren't so kind. *Sun News* is using the incident as another example of out-of-control metahumans and calling for military intervention, warning that US-based metahumans, like me, are breaking international laws that could lead to World War III.

Newly depressed, I switch over to the contacts app and find Derrick's number as I exit the building.

"Hey, Connor, one second," Derrick says on the other end.

The sounds of the busy newsroom fade as Derrick steps into his office and closes the door.

"I can't talk long, busy day," Derrick says.

"Yeah, I'm aware."

"Did Michelle talk to you?"

"Yeah."

"Look, the reactor exploding wasn't your fault. You did your best and prevented significant loss of life."

"For now."

"*For now* is the best we can ever hope for sometimes. No one knows what will happen in the future. Maybe there will be a scientific breakthrough, and everyone will be back in their homes before we know it."

"A scientific breakthrough that speeds up the half-life of plutonium from twenty-four thousand years to two?"

"Look, you know better than most that stranger things have happened."

The noise from the newsroom spills back into the room as someone enters Derrick's office.

"Sorry, Connor, I've got to go. You'll be okay, though, I promise."

Before I can respond, there's a click and Derrick is gone.

I sigh and pocket my phone. As I walk up the hill to the dormitories, I spot Sarah walking toward me with someone I've never seen before. They're almost on top of me before Sarah looks away long enough to notice.

"Oh, hey Connor," Sarah says.

"Hey, Sarah."

"Coming back from detention?"

"Huh? No. I didn't have detention today."

"You didn't? I must have heard wrong. Something about Mr. Muldowney's class and you leaving early to... something. I don't know. I forget."

Great. Not only is Omni public enemy number one, but the entire school knows about my improvised "stomach issues." If Sarah, who isn't in Mr. Muldowney's class, thinks

I had detention, then it's a sure sign I've got it coming next time I see him.

"Oh yeah, that. I think it's fine. Me and Muldowney are buddies," I say, lying through my teeth.

"Okay," Sarah replies, not knowing how to continue the conversation after bringing up rumors about my bowels.

Despite her initial excitement over joining the metahuman training program, Sarah has since decided against it. I think she just doesn't want to spend time with me, which she would have to do in the training program. Her official reason is she's not actually a metahuman: she simply had access to Midnight's mech suit and did what anyone else would have done when she stepped in to help fight the Alphas.

Everyone knows that isn't true. She'd stepped up because it was the right thing to do and she was brave enough to do it. Those are the qualities Michelle and Midnight look for in people they want to admit into the program, metahuman or not.

At first, Sarah took the news I was a metahuman well, all things considered. But once the shock wore off, she realized I'd been lying to her since last summer, when I'd found my metabands. I told her I'd done it to keep her safe, but she didn't see it that way, nor did she think she needed me to keep her safe. I couldn't really argue with that.

She told me she thought we should take some time apart, even as friends. I never intended for her to get mixed up in the metahuman world, and I understood her need to distance herself from it. I wish things were different, but unfortunately for me, granting wishes isn't one of my powers.

I glance over at her friend. He's tall, or taller than me, with dark hair shaved on the sides and long enough on top that his bangs cover half his face. He's wearing somewhat plain clothes, jeans and a black sweatshirt. Despite the fact they're plain they look expensive. They're cut like they were tailored to him. He barely glances up from his phone as Sarah and I talk.

"Oh, I'm being rude. Connor, this is Kyle. He's in the after-school robotics club with me. Kyle, this is Connor. He and I went to the same school together."

Went to the same school together?

We dated for... all right, I guess we didn't date for that long, but still. That's *something*. Certainly it's more relevant than being classmates. I don't expect her to tell him we've saved each other's lives a handful of times, just something more than we went to the same school together. Heck, we still go to the same school, so it's obviously no big deal.

I reach out and shake Kyle's hand. His grip is hard, maybe too hard. He stares me dead in the eye, unblinking, as he shakes but says nothing. I offer a polite, "nice to meet you," but he doesn't reciprocate. There's a brief awkward silence.

"I'm sorry, Conrad. My mind is elsewhere. It's nice to meet you."

"Connor."

"Pardon?"

"It's Connor, not Conrad."

"Of course, my apologies. As I mentioned, my mind is elsewhere."

I glance at Sarah to read her face, but there's nothing there. I can't tell if this guy is always like this or he's acting like a jerk.

"We gotta get going, sorry. Good to see you, Connor," Sarah offers with a slight wave before they continue on their way.

Now she's the one saying polite things she doesn't mean. As they walk away, Kyle suddenly becomes talkative.

"Where was I again?" he asks Sarah. "Oh, right, the gyroscopic interface. I've been doing some research, and I think..."

They drift out of my normal hearing range, but it doesn't sound like a conversation worth firing up my metabands over, even if I wasn't expressly forbidden from using them.

SIX

It's a quiet walk the rest of the way to my dorm room. It's dinnertime and campus is empty as the sun goes down. I open the door to my room and nearly jump out of my skin when I find it's not empty.

"Ah!" Jim yells in response to my yell. Instinctively, he slams shut the notebook computer perched on his lap. "Nothing!" he shouts in response to a question I didn't ask.

Jim moved in a few weeks ago, and the difference between him and my previous roommate is like night and day. I mean that literally. Jim is a borderline insomniac, or at least nocturnal. The only thing he loves more than his computer is food, which is why I'm surprised he's here instead of at the dining hall.

After Jim nearly got himself killed working on the same side as the Alphas, I worried it would take a while for us to get back on speaking terms, let alone become friends again. I underestimated how much both of us almost dying would speed up the process. His views on metahumans changed when he saw what the bad ones could do. He even got over the fact I had kept my metabands a secret from him. His admittance into Skyville Academy and getting to occasionally help Midnight might have softened him up on that front.

"It's fine, Jim. I know you're reading about the disaster in Japan," I say as I empty my pockets and place my keys and wallet on my desk.

"Just catching up on the fallout," he says. "Oh, jeez, no, not like *fallout* fallout. That's a poor choice of words. I meant, I'm catching up on all the different metahumans and governments mad at you."

"That doesn't make me feel better. How bad is it?"

"It's bad, if you want the honest truth."

"And if I don't want the honest truth?"

"Then it's fine. Everything is fine."

"Great, that puts my mind at ease."

I close the door, plop down on my narrow bed, and take a long exaggerated sigh as I stare up at the ceiling.

"Um, so how was the rest of your day?" Jim asks.

"Michelle revoked my metaband use on campus."

"Yeah, I heard about that. She kinda chewed me out too. No metabands to threaten me with, but she reminded me she pulled the strings to get me here, and if I ever provide comms support during class again, we'll be having another conversation that won't be as friendly."

"You were in class while you were talking me through a nuclear reactor meltdown?"

"I wasn't in class, just a lab."

"Oh, that's much better."

"Better than pretending I'm about to crap my pants just to get out."

I glare at Jim.

"Sorry, too soon?" he says.

"I saw Sarah today."

"Oh... how was that?"

"It was fine. Okay, it was weird. She pretended like she barely knew me, called me someone she used to go to school with."

"She didn't exactly take the news you're a metahuman all that well."

"I know, but I was hoping, I don't know, she'd eventually get over it and things would go back to normal."

"And what is *normal* for us?"

"You've got a point. I probably shouldn't give it much thought. We've been broken up for months, and she wants to move on with her life. She doesn't owe it to me to keep me a part of it, right?"

"Wow, how mature of you, Connor. And here I thought you could only turn into an adult by clicking those fancy bracelets together. I'm proud of you."

I take the pillow from under my head and fling it at Jim as hard as I can.

"Hey, watch it! This laptop technically belongs to the school, you know. I've gotta give it back in one piece at the end of the semester."

"You know Midnight will make you drill a hole through the hard drive since you've been using it to help me, right?"

"What!" Jim says.

"Sarah was with some guy," I mention, shifting the subject abruptly.

"Oh? Maybe it was just a friend or something."

"That's what she said. Someone from her robotics club."

"Kyle?"

My heart plummets. Jim must know who he is because Kyle and Sarah are more than just friends. Jim still talks to Sarah a lot. If she is seeing someone new, there's a good chance he'd know about it.

"Yeah," I whisper.

"Oh! No, I didn't mean it that way. You think I know his name because they're together or something, but it's way crazier than that. I know his name because he's probably the richest kid at an already rich school."

"How come I haven't heard about him, then?"

"Uh, probably because you spend every waking minute figuring out how to sneak out of class to go put on tights instead of paying attention."

"They're not tights."

"I know they're not tights. It's a figure of speech."

"Is it?"

"Anyway, Kyle. Yeah, he's the super insanely rich kid. No one is supposed to know who he is, but there are tons of crazy rumors. Mark down the hall says he heard he's Albert Einstein's secret son."

"I hope I don't have to explain how impossible that is."

"I dunno. He uses a fake last name. I heard there are undercover bodyguards disguised as students following him around all the time."

"Unless Sarah's been secretly training as an undercover bodyguard, I don't think that's true either."

"Hey man, I'm just updating you on the rumors. Supposedly, he's a genius too."

"Great, an insanely rich genius. I don't know what Sarah could ever see in him."

"He's good looking too. I mean, that's what I heard."

"Opsec."

"Huh?"

"Opsec. Operational security. That's what Midnight calls it. Leave no trace and all that. He probably would have already drilled a hole through your laptop if he knew you were using school property to assist me with meta-y things."

"You're exaggerating. I mean, he'd buy me a new one, wouldn't he?"

"I dunno. You'd have to ask him, not me. But I wouldn't ask him, since then, you know, he'd know you have it and then..." I make a drilling noise and mime holding a power drill.

"I really like this laptop."

"I'm sure you do. Speaking of Midnight, I should get going. Michelle said he wants to speak with me tonight."

"Oh no, he wants to talk about the meltdown? Do you think you can skip it? Pretend you forgot?"

I stare at Jim, who should know better.

"Yeah," he says, "that's probably not a great idea."

"According to Michelle, it isn't about that."

"Oh..." Jim says as he flips open his laptop again.

"What are you doing?"

"Seeing what else is going on in the world and checking the latest Midnight sightings. There's gotta be a clue somewhere. Keeping track of him got way harder after your brother's website stopped posting sightings of him regularly."

"I think it was the least my brother could do after Midnight saved my life a few times. Derrick said the Midnight sightings page wasn't getting anywhere near as many page views as it used to before metabands started working again, so it wasn't that tough of a decision."

"Where are you meeting him?"

"Don't know yet."

On cue, my phone pings with a message.

"Speak of the devil," I say.

"He has this placed bugged, doesn't he?" Jim asks sincerely.

"Nah, I don't think so. Probably just a coincidence."

"I'm sleeping with my laptop under my pillow tonight—just in case."

After authenticating my identity with a facial scan, fingerprint scan, and a unique password, the message unlocks.

The message contains coordinates with no further instructions. Midnight likes to keep things simple whenever possible.

"When are you meeting him?" Jim asks.

"It doesn't say."

"If it doesn't say, how do you know when you should be there?"

"In my experience, if there isn't a time listed in his message, that means the meeting time is now."

I sit up in my bed and notice how I haven't been home long enough to kick my shoes off yet.

"What time will you be back?" Jim asks.

"Don't worry, I won't ask you to wait up for me."

"It's not that. It's just, um, you remember that Muldowney's giving a quiz tomorrow, don't you?"

Crap. I hadn't remembered. Jim isn't in my class; otherwise, I would have asked him to create a distraction instead of humiliating myself, but he has Muldowney earlier in the day. Ironically, Jim is one of his favorite students. Just add "failing a test" to the pile of things Muldowney can be mad at me about tomorrow.

"I'll study when I get back."

"Are you sure you'll be back so soon? I mean, the guy's name is Midnight for a reason."

"I'll figure it out. I'd much rather deal with Muldowney's wrath than Midnight's."

"Good point."

I'm back onto my feet, stuffing my wallet and keys back into my pockets.

"How are you getting there?" Jim asks.

"What do you mean? What's wrong with the ol' activate the metabands up on the roof?"

A few weeks ago, Jim helped me get a duplicate key for the rooftop access door. Our dorm is one of the taller building on campus, making it impossible for anyone to see our rooftop from any nearby building. Having rooftop access has made activating my metabands and launching into the night sky much, much easier.

"Um, Michelle's rule?"

"Dammit, right. That probably only applies during school hours?"

"If you want to tell yourself that, go ahead, but we both know that's not what she meant."

Jim's right.

I sigh. "I'll figure it out, I guess."

SEVEN

I wait until after dinner to escape campus. Besides the ban on using my metabands while on campus grounds, there's another wrinkle: leaving campus after 8:00 p.m. requires special permission. You would think teenagers would be itching to break this rule constantly, but you'd be wrong for one simple reason: there's nothing to do in town.

What passes for Main Street in Skyville isn't far down the road, but it offers exceedingly little in the way of fun, especially nighttime fun. Sure, occasionally you hear of seniors' elaborate plans to sneak down the road and paint the town red and use fake IDs to get into the only hole-in-the-wall bar for fifty miles, but things rarely go as planned. Usually, the local police escort the seniors back to campus roughly ten minutes after they walk into the bar, which hasn't seen a new face walk through the doors in over a decade.

Sneaking off campus at night isn't that difficult; it's just a pain in the butt that's rarely worth the effort. Normally, I go to the roof or walk half a mile into the woods, activate my metabands, and call it a day. But while that *should* be fine, the woods are technically part of school property, and if there's one thing I know about Michelle, it's that she's a stickler for details, and she somehow has eyes everywhere. It just isn't worth the risk of getting caught.

The quickest way off campus is the simplest: right through the front gates. I approach the main entrance cautiously. There won't be many vehicles coming or going, except for staff and faculty. That means only one guard is on duty, and I can see him sitting in the booth, watching a small TV on his desk.

I approach the gate hoping if I move slowly enough, he won't notice me slip by. This plan lasts approximately five seconds before a set of headlights send me diving into a shrub.

I crash through the branches and pull my legs in. Once I'm sure no one can see me, I carefully push branches out of the way.

The gate to the campus slowly rises into the air. I think little of the car, assuming it'll breeze right through, but it stops in front of the wide-open gate.

The guard stands from his desk and walks out the door of the tiny shack to speak with the driver. Peering through the driver's side window, I see it's Muldowney in the car. The guard approaches the passenger side window, which Mr. Muldowney rolls down. The guard smiles as he leans over and rests his arms against the car's frame.

Great. They're buddies. Of course they are. They both love busting people's chops. My right leg is falling asleep because of the weird angle I'm sitting at, and I wonder if these two blabbermouths are planning on spending the entire night out here catching up on... whatever teachers and security guards like to talk about.

Just when I think it's time to get out of this bush and

think of another plan, the guard straightens back up and the car pulls forward and exits the campus. The guard returns toward his gatehouse shack, turning his back to me.

It's now or never.

I claw my way out of the shrub, mindful not to make too much noise that might attract the guard's attention. Once I'm out, I spring to my feet, only to discover that my right leg is almost entirely asleep. I try to ignore it and tell my leg to move, but it's clumsy and awkward.

The guard is turning the doorknob to the gatehouse as I struggle to turn my limp into a jog. I catch a break when the guard realizes the shanty door must have locked behind him when he exited. He fishes a massive set of keys attached to a large metallic ring out of his pocket and fingers through the keys.

I catch another small break when he drops them. The guard quietly curses as he bends over to retrieve them. This is the best chance I'll get, so I hoof it as fast as I can with a dead leg.

I make it outside the gate just as the guard pushes the right key into the lock and enters the guardhouse. Behind me, the mechanical gate rumbles closed.

I did it.

I jog farther down the road to make sure I'm far enough away from the guard or any cars that might come in or out. Confident I'm out of sight, I turn right and head about ten yards into the surrounding forest before summoning my metabands with a flick of my wrists.

I activate the bands, and it only takes a near-subconscious thought to cause the crimson uniform to flow out and cover my body.

Now it's time to find Midnight.

EIGHT

Hovering over Bay View City, I try to work out the location of Midnight's coordinates. I've never been great at finding locations without a map and he wants me to get better at not always having to rely on them. Couldn't he just give me a landmark or something? I'm halfway to the city's financial district when my comms clicks on.

"Why would you think those coordinates are for Lincoln Tower?" Midnight asks over the two-way communication device.

"How on earth can you possibly know where I'm heading?" I ask.

"You're wearing a bright red costume and flying two thousand feet above the city. Not that hard."

He's got me there.

"You're also late."

"Sorry, it's not easy to get off campus in a hurry when I'm not allowed to use my metabands."

There's a grumble on the other side of the earpiece.

"Now will have to do then. Meet me at the Hampshire Bridge, northbound side," Midnight says.

The comms clicks off before I can respond. I'm used to it, though. Midnight's all about keeping unnecessary communication to a minimum over the air. According to him, it'd take something like ten billion years to break the wireless encryption on our comms, but that doesn't mean it's impossible.

I pivot 360 degrees in the air, looking for the bridge. It's easy to get disorientated at this height, but I spot the red lights dotting the suspension cables, which ensure that low-flying planes don't accidentally crash into it in the middle of the night.

I approach the bridge cautiously since I don't know anything about the situation or why Midnight is there. The last thing I want to do today is screw something else up by jumping in headfirst. I land on the tallest support cable to keep a lower profile while I scan the bridge for any sign of him.

As soon as I land, I hear him come up behind me.

"Good, you found me," he says.

I had no idea he was up here. I just chose the tallest point, but I'm not about to correct him.

"Yup, I knew you'd be here. It makes sense."

Midnight doesn't respond.

Probably laid it on too thick there.

"Um, anyway, Michelle said you wanted to talk?" I say.

"Yes... hold on a minute."

He crouches and puts a pair of binoculars I didn't notice he was holding up to his eyes. His head remains perfectly still, his sights trained on something in the distance.

"False alarm," he declares and stands to face me.

"What's going on?" I ask.

"There's a shipment of deactivated metabands coming

through here tonight, and I have intel that someone's going to try to rob it."

"What do you mean *deactivated*?"

"They're from before," he says.

"If they're from the first wave, then aren't they useless? They don't even work for their original owners anymore."

"Just because they won't power on doesn't mean they're entirely useless. If that were true, the government wouldn't be moving them from the Natural History Museum to a secure location."

"That's weird."

"It is. Whoever is planning to knock over the truck might also be responsible for the move. Regardless of their motivation, it's not a good idea to let the bands fall into the wrong hands, even if they're inert."

"And I'm here as backup? To help you out?"

"No. You're an hour late to a meeting that has nothing to do with this. You should have been on your way back home by now."

"Oh, okay."

Midnight picks his binoculars up and begins scanning the far end of the bridge.

"How familiar are you with robotics?"

"I took on that crazy giant robot guy the one time. Remember that?"

"Not how good are you at fighting them, but how good are you at building them?"

"At building robots? You want me to help you build a robot?"

Midnight sighs.

"Just answer the questions. After that, you can ask me whatever you'd like."

I note he said I can *ask* him whatever I'd like, not he'd *answer* any questions.

"Sorry."

"Do you think you can get up to speed fast enough that it wouldn't seem ridiculous for you to join the robotics team at your school?"

"You want me to apply for the robotics team?"

"You won't have to apply. Michelle will see you're approved to join the team. My question is: Can you become knowledgeable enough in a short period of time that it won't raise any unnecessary eyebrows?"

"How soon are we talking?"

"Tomorrow."

"Tomorrow? Uh, I mean, I guess I can read a couple of articles about robotics by then."

"There won't be a quiz on the first day. Michelle will get you some literature so you can familiarize yourself with enough of the terminology so you're not completely lost."

"Okay, that still doesn't explain why you want me to join the robotics team. Do you want me to start designing gadgets for you or something?"

Midnight glares at me.

"Right, hold all my questions until the end. I forgot."

Then it hits me how awkward it'll seem when I suddenly decided to join the robotics team, a subject I have no interest in, less than twenty-four hours after running into my ex-girlfriend and her new guy friend. I consider expressing my concern, then promptly remember that it's the last thing he would ever care about.

"If this is a punch-bad-guys-in-the-face type of operation, you should know that Michelle threatened to have me expelled if I use my metabands on campus again without her okay."

"She informed me."

Of course she did.

"This is a different type of mission."

"Finally, you guys want to use me for my dazzling personality instead of my superpowers. I knew you'd eventually come around."

Midnight doesn't even bother to glare at me for that one.

"The academy's robotics team has been invited to the Wichita Meadows Advanced Testing Facility. It's a secure government facility. The cover story is they're working on the future of robotics, but I have intel that says otherwise. We need you to go on that trip to get to the bottom of the type of research being done there."

"And punch some bad guys?"

"To observe and report."

"Sounds thrilling."

Midnight pulls out his binoculars again and trains them on a far-off target. Seconds later, he lowers them.

"If you follow the instructions I give you it will be anything but thrilling, but the information you get will be useful to us. What do you know about Kaldonia?"

"Uh, I've steered clear because of the urban legend that metabands don't work there. It's supposed to be a Bermuda Triangle type place for them. Never seemed worth it to test that theory since I'm rarely in that part of the world anyway."

"It's not an urban legend. Metabands cannot activate within a five-hundred-mile radius of the capital city."

"Whoa, really? These things work in outer space, but you're telling me they don't work in this country? How?"

"We're not sure, but we'd like to find out. The country has been under dictatorships since its founding seventy years ago. Little information comes out of the country and presumably even less gets in. We believe scientists at the Wichita Meadows facility may have reverse-engineered the technology Kaldonia is using to keep metahumans out of their country. This trip is a rare opportunity to glean first-hand evidence of what might be going on there. I've been trying to get close for a while and this field trip is as good a chance as we'll get."

"Um, if it's a top-secret facility, aren't they probably going to keep a bunch of students away from all the top-secret stuff?"

"That's likely, but it doesn't mean there won't be other information to gather."

"I ran into Sarah today, and she was with a guy who's also on the robotics team. Does that have anything to do with this?"

"Yes. Kyle Toslov is the son of the Mikah Akulov, the president of Kaldonia."

"What? Really? Why does he have a different last name, though?"

"He has more than a different name; his entire identity is fictional."

"I knew something was off about him."

"He's not a subject of interest at this time. The false identity is simply a cover while he attends school in the United States. Without it, any family member of Akulov, especially offspring, could become a target to those with an ax to grind with the Kaldonian government."

"I'll still keep an eye on him."

"No, you're to maintain your cover at all costs. If your cover is blown, it could jeopardize the entire operation."

"Fine, I'll mind my own business," I sigh.

"Good. The bus leaves tomorrow night in order to get to

Wichita Meadows in the morning. Remember, no one outside of the robotics team knows about the trip. It is imperative you act surprised when you're told."

"Got it, no problem. I'm a fantastic actor."

Midnight turns to look at me.

"Don't oversell it."

"Got it. Cool as a cucumber. They won't even think I want to go on the trip."

Midnight grumbles. It wasn't worth arguing. He lifts the binoculars to his eyes again. At first, I think this is his way of changing the subject, but something's got his attention.

"This is it. Stay here," Midnight says as he folds the binoculars flat and tucks them into a compartment on his belt.

"Huh?" I barely get out before he's gone.

NINE

Midnight plummets toward the road in a swan dive before launching a grappling hook into a support beam and swinging into a wide arc.

Underneath him on the road, a semi-trailer truck is cruising over the bridge. Unbeknownst to the driver, five identical black motorcycles are moving into position, two on either side and one behind. If these aren't the hijackers, then their fashion choices are surprisingly well coordinated.

Midnight lands on the trailer's roof with the lightness of a cat. He swiftly reloads the grappling gun before firing it at the motorcycle behind the truck. The hook flies through the back tire, and the guideline wraps around the wheel, causing it to seize. The motorcycle and its rider tumble across the highway. The car behind him on the road skids to a stop, narrowly missing the rider.

Midnight reloads another grappling hook. He turns and fires it into the sky ahead of the truck. It wraps around one of the bridge's supports and locks into place. Without hesitation, Midnight leaps off the truck and kicks a motorcycle rider off his bike before retracting the line to catch back up with and land on the roof of the tractor-trailer.

On the far side of the truck, I hear the roar of a bike's engine, followed by a loud metallic scraping. Once the truck is out of the way, I can see a rider-less motorcycle skidding across the bridge. There's movement in the truck's cab.

It's the rider who ditched his motorcycle in an attempt to commandeer the truck. Before I can decide whether or not to help, Midnight is on top of the cab, pulling the rider out through the passenger window before he can reach the driver. He attaches one end of a grappling line to the rider's belt and fires the other end at one of the bridge's suspension cables. The line goes taut and launches the rider into the air, leaving him dangling above traffic.

Too late, I notice the two remaining riders have sped up in front the truck and stopped their bikes, creating a small barricade. This wouldn't normally stop a truck this size, except the men are holding machine guns at their sides.

The driver slams on the brakes and the truck screeches to a halt before Midnight can turn to notice them, sending him tumbling into the air. He lands directly between the stopped semi truck and the two gunmen.

Police sirens wail in the distance, growing louder.

Midnight has found himself in a vulnerable position: on his back while two armed men approach. They raise their guns and take aim.

My feet hit the pavement. They squeeze the trigger and ammunition rains from the guns at a rate of a dozen bullets per second. I know because I count the bullets as they hit my chest and bounce off, landing in a growing pile at my feet.

The magazines run out, and the men realize that instead of executing Midnight, they've just unloaded their guns into a metahuman, who swooped down between them and their target faster than it took the first bullet to leave the chamber.

They stumble and disengage their empty magazines as they reach for the ammunition on their belts.

I'm behind them quicker than their eyes can perceive and waste no time. Grabbing them by the backs of their jacket collars, I smash their helmeted heads together. I release them, and they crumple to the ground, knocked out cold and their helmets cracked.

The traffic on the bridge has completely stopped with some drivers trying to turn around to avoid the scene.

"I told you to wait," Midnight grumbles.

"You're welcome," I reply.

"I had it handled."

"I got bored waiting up there for you to finish."

Midnight limps to the driver's side of the truck and talks with the driver. After he steps back, the driver shifts gears and the truck rolls forward to continue its journey over the bridge.

"He's not waiting for the police to arrive?" I ask.

"No point. It's more important he get the shipment where it's going than give the police a statement about a bunch of motorcycle henchmen."

"Yeah, but—"

Before I can finish my thought, he fires a grappling hook high above the bridge and rockets into the air.

I shake my head and follow him back to his perch.

"We'll wait up here until the cops come. The people in their cars are likely starting to post photos of the scene. You especially don't need that kind of attention right now."

"Thanks for that."

Midnight jumps back into our earlier conversation as

though he didn't just swan dive off a suspension bridge and take on five gunmen by himself.

Well, almost by himself.

"I've spoken to your brother earlier today. He'll be joining you on the trip as a chaperone."

"What? He wouldn't even chaperone my class visit to the zoo in third grade because he said it would eat up too much of his day, but now he's willing to spend fourteen hours on a bus?"

"He's a journalist. He jumped at the chance to visit a secure facility."

"Yeah, that sounds like him. Nothing like complicating your spy mission with a little investigative journalism. We'll be lucky if they even let us in."

"They are aware of who Derrick is. He's been given an exclusive on what the group will be shown tomorrow with the stipulation his article cannot go to press until next week. Still, both of you will keep a low profile. Kaldonia isn't yet a threat; it's simply a place of interest. If it's true metabands don't work there and the US government has figured out why, then we want to know too. The country is producing power at unprecedented levels. Intel tells us this energy isn't coming from fossil fuels or nuclear sources."

"Solar or wind?"

"At the scale they're producing energy, we would see it on satellite imagery if it were coming from a green source. There are rumors that they're looking to sell their excess energy to neighboring nations. It could be connected to the country's metaband immunity or it could not be, but that's why you're going on this fact-finding mission. On that note, there is another stipulation to this trip. You have to leave your metabands here."

"Wait, I have to leave my metabands hundreds of miles

away while I'm undercover in a top-secret government facility? What if something happens? What if I need them?"

"If you need them, then you've failed your mission."

"I'd still feel more comfortable having them and not using them, then not having them at all."

"I understand. There's a draw to them—a connection."

Midnight looks down at his arm, the one that was severed with a metaband still attached. He flexes his gloved fingers.

"Losing your metabands, even temporarily, makes you feel like something is wrong and adds a general unease to every situation. I get it. But we can't risk it. We're not sure what you might encounter at this facility."

Midnight knows I'm beginning to appreciate the full weight of what's he's asking me to do and doesn't push further. He understands me well enough to know that I sometimes need a minute to think, even when I already know the answer.

"Okay, I'll keep them here."

"I knew you'd understand. This is not small thing we're asking you to do, Connor. There's significant risk. I'd understand if you refused to go, and I'm sure Derrick would understand too."

I laugh.

"No, he wouldn't."

I can almost see a smirk cross Midnight's face. He knows Derrick would never turn down a chance like this, regardless of the risk.

"We'll be out of contact during your trip. It's not worth the risk of smuggling your comms into the base. Even if you got it past the security checkpoint, the facility is shielded against outside radio waves. It would be easy for them to pick up any attempt to breach that shield and trace it back to you."

"Got it. No phone calls while I'm there either. Any other restrictions? Can I bring my wallet or play it safe and buy one in the gift shop after I'm there?"

"You'll follow me back to one of my outposts," Midnight says, ignoring my smart-ass question. "Once we're there, you can deactivate your metabands and leave them in my care. I'll keep them safe."

"How will I get back to campus, then? Can I borrow some cool, tricked-out car you have hidden in a garage somewhere in the city?"

"No, but I'll cover your cab fare."

It was worth a try.

TEN

Today is rushed and chaotic. Part of me is grateful. It means I haven't had time to think too much about how risky this trip is.

Adding to the chaos is the fact I can't skip any of my regularly scheduled classes, including the quiz in Muldowney's class that I definitely failed. I've missed so many classes even Michelle couldn't clear my schedule, and the administration office made it clear I must make up all the work I've missed over the weekend, no exceptions.

Between my classes, I've been heading back to my room to pack. Since I'm a last-minute addition to the trip, no one has given me any instructions on what to bring. The thought crosses my mind to ask Jim for help since he's also coming, but he's busy with his own preparations. Plus, I remember the story of when Jim's family let him pack his own luggage for a family vacation to Wilson World. He forgot to pack underwear.

Not that I want Jim riffling through my underwear drawer.

As I'm heading back to my dorm room for the third time

today, thinking about how I'd love to steal ten minutes to run to the dining hall, I glance down at my phone and find a voicemail from Derrick. I tap the message and put the phone to my ear. Ten seconds tick by before Derrick talks. He obviously became distracted while listening to my voicemail greeting.

"Hey Connor. It's Derrick. You know that already. Just calling to, um—"

I'm familiar with Derrick drifting off like this. Usually, it means he got a message on his computer that he absentmindedly started reading instead of finishing his thought. After five seconds of silence, I consider hanging up and calling him since that might be quicker.

"Sorry, got distracted there. Anyway, I was calling to see how the packing is going. I haven't even started mine yet. Still lots of news today about… well, you know. Anyway, I'll be stuck here for a bit, so I'll just meet you at the academy tonight. See you there. Exciting stuff!"

Click.

Derrick isn't on his way to winning "chaperone of the year" by any stretch of the imagination.

I unlock the door to my dorm room and find Jim hefting a backpack onto his shoulders. Next to him is a large rolling suitcase.

"There you are!" he says. "Jeez, I thought you were going to miss the bus. Ready to roll out?"

"Roll out? The bus doesn't leave until five p.m.?"

"The bus leaves at four."

"Four? Okay, okay, just give me two minutes," I say in a panic as I shove items into a duffel bag.

"We don't have two minutes, Connor. We're already late. Just grab what you can. You can buy whatever you need when we get there."

"I thought the facility was isolated?"

"It is. I'm lying to you. We need to go."

"Fine, fine. Let's go."

I close the half-filled duffel bag and follow Jim into the hallway. He locks the door, which is great, because that's something I totally would have forgotten to do.

"They wouldn't leave without us, right?" I ask.

"I'm not sure," Jim says. "I'd rather not find out."

"Me neither."

I take two steps down the hall before Jim grabs my arm.

"This way," he says.

"Right."

Outside the dormitory, as we're trekking across the lawn, Jim dragging his suitcases behind, the wheels stubbornly refusing to roll in the grass, he scans the area to make sure no one is in hearing range.

"Dude, what the heck is going on? How are you going on this trip? Do you even know anything about robotics?"

"Why does everyone keep asking me that? It's like you all forgot about that giant robot I fought—no, the giant robot I *beat*."

"You know we're not going there to fight robots, right?"

"It may come up."

"For your sake, I hope it doesn't. I can't even imagine the storm you'd bring down on your head if you sparked up your metabands at a secure government research facility."

"Thanks for the vote of confidence, Jim, but I'm leaving my metabands behind."

"No way."

"Yes way, look."

I put my wrist out and mentally try to summon my metabands. Nothing happens.

"Um, so you think showing me your bare wrists proves you don't have them?" Jim says.

"No, I'm trying to summon them to prove I don't have them."

"Okay, that doesn't prove anything, but I believe you. Just hope we don't run into any trouble where you might need them."

"You just said I shouldn't use them!"

"Yeah, but better to have them and not need them than to need them and not have them."

"It's a two-day trip. I should be fine."

"I still don't understand how you got added last minute."

"Michelle pulled some strings."

"Why would she do that? You aren't just going on this trip because Sarah and Kyle are, are you?"

"What? No, of course not. That'd be insane."

"Okay, good."

We trudge down the hill toward the student union, where we're meeting the rest of the team. I decide to tell Jim why I'm really going before we're surrounded with other students.

"Midnight wants me to do reconnaissance."

"What!" Jim yells, and I instinctively look around to make sure no one can overhear us. Jim lowers his voice, barely, but doesn't hide how upset he is. "You're going to Wichita Meadows to do reconnaissance for Midnight? Reconnaissance of what? What if they catch you? What if they catch *me*?"

"Well, you're not doing anything wrong, so they won't catch you doing anything."

"That's what you think, but you don't know how the

legal system works. They could claim I was your accomplice!"

"You usually are my accomplice."

"That's not funny, Connor. They could throw us in some government prison where no one will ever hear from us again."

"That won't happen. Probably. It'll be fine. I don't even have a defined mission. Observe and report, that's all."

"You'll be lucky if Muldowney even lets you do that much."

"Wait, why would Muldowney have anything to do with it?"

"Uh, because he's the robotics coach."

I stop dead in my tracks.

"Muldowney is the robotics coach? Why didn't anyone tell me?" I ask, coming close to yelling myself.

"Why didn't anyone tell you? I didn't even know you were on the team until this morning."

"That's because you were already asleep when I got home last night!"

"Yeah, because I had a big day to get ready for!"

We arrive at the bottom of the hill and see the bus idling outside the student union. Both of us lower our voices.

"Muldowney hates me. He won't be happy that I'm on this trip."

"Duh."

As we approach the bus, the accordion-style door folds open, and Muldowney steps off the bus.

"Just under the wire, boys. Bus was just about to leave. Come on, hustle up," Muldowney says as we approach, reminding me of my other least favorite thing about him: his out-of-context use of sports metaphors and sayings. We really are late if the rest of the team has already boarded the bus.

"Sorry we're late. I couldn't find my charger," Jim offers by way of apology.

Muldowney looks right through him, focusing his glare on me instead.

"Connolly. So nice of you to join us. And I mean that literally since I only learned of your deep-seated love of all things robotics this afternoon. I have a Derrick Connolly on my list here as a chaperone. Your father, I assume?"

"No, he's my brother."

"There are two of you? And I thought I pitied your parents before," he says with a smirk.

I didn't expect him to know my parents are dead. It's a big school with lots of students. But I thought he would have picked up on the clue my brother is chaperoning because there might be more to the story here. That, however, would require Muldowney to think about someone other than himself for half a second. He might not have intended to sound so harsh, but he succeeded in making me mad, and I'll be damned if I give him the satisfaction of showing it.

"He should be here any second," I say.

"Any second, huh? Was he aware when he signed up as a chaperone he'd be required to be around the individuals he's meant to supervise?"

"He knows. He'll be here."

I can feel my face flushing. If my metabands weren't locked away somewhere, they might have started to rematerialize from the emotional reaction I'm fighting hard to repress.

Jim pushes me toward the bus, saying in hushed tones, "Just get on the bus. He's just trying to rattle you."

"What was that, James?" Muldowney asks.

"Nothing. I was just telling Connor to get on the bus before it leaves without us."

"Good thinking, Mr. Young." Muldowney puts a hand out to stop me from entering the bus but waves at Jim to keep going.

Jim hesitates but ultimately listens.

Muldowney brings his head in close to mine. "I don't know who the hell you or your brother know that got you on this trip, but let me tell you, I do not appreciate it. The rest of these kids worked hard all semester. They earned this trip, and I will not let someone who has wandered in off the street ruin it. I'm keeping an eye on you, Connolly, and don't think I won't send you home in a heartbeat if I think you're jeopardizing their experience. Capisce?"

"Yeah, I got it," I say.

ELEVEN

Once on the bus, I make my way toward the row Jim has taken a seat in when Muldowney shouts from behind me.

"Where do you think you are going, Mr. Connolly? There are assigned seats on this trip. You're in G1."

So much for sitting with Jim. I look up at the seat numbers printed above each row and make my way backward toward row G where I find a surprise waiting for me: I'm sitting right next to Kyle.

"Hey," I say as I approach him.

He's sitting in the aisle seat of a two-seater row. He doesn't respond or even acknowledge me. I point to the window seat.

"I think that's my seat."

He finally looks up, but instead of getting up to let me by, he barely moves his legs. Instead of pressing the issue, I awkwardly squeeze past his legs and flop into my seat.

At the front of the bus, I see a harried figure clomping up the stairs.

It's Derrick, of course.

I'm glad he's here, although judging by the state he's

in—shirt untucked, hair disheveled —it looks like he barely made it. He waves as he passes my seat and explains he's off in the back. Before I can suggest switching seats with whoever is seated next to him, he's gone.

Kyle and I sit quietly as the door to the bus closes and the driver shifts it into gear.

I wonder if Kyle and I will sit in total silence the entire way there.

Finally, I break the ice.

"So, how long have you been on the robotics team?"

"Longer than you have," he replies.

I laugh, playing off the comment.

"Ha, yeah. I had no idea they'd be sending me on a trip like this on my first official day in the club."

"I'm sure you didn't." Kyle's tone heavily implies he's not being sincere. Before I can change the subject, Kyle asks, "So, what are your feelings about Kaldonia?"

This throws me for a loop. I doubt he knows that I know who he really is, but the question implies he might.

"I'm not sure," I say. "I guess it's a complicated subject."

"It's not that complicated, actually. It mostly comes down to whether you believe a nation has the right to ban metahumans."

"That's the complicated part."

"Ah, so you support metahumans."

"Metahumans are like anyone else. They just happen to have abilities outside our general understanding of physics."

"You say that like it's a minor issue."

"Obviously, it's not, but metahumans aren't automatically good or bad. The metabands kinda shine a light on who the person really is."

"Power tends to do that."

"I'm not sure what the solution is, but if a country decides they don't want them, it's up to them, really."

"We'll just have to agree to disagree, I suppose."

"Wait, what? You're pro-metahuman?"

"I don't know if I would say that, but I don't believe they should be banned from a nation entirely."

"But I thought you were..."

"The son of Mikah Akulov?"

We're barely into the bus ride and I've already blown the fact that I know who he is. This trip is going great so far.

"I mean, I heard a rumor about that, but I didn't necessar—"

"No, it's true. I've done my best to keep it under wraps, but there's only so much one can do, even in a place as large as the academy, to keep such a big secret."

"So, you're okay with people knowing who you are?"

"Yes. It was my father's decision to enroll me under an assumed identity. It's the product of his paranoia and one of the concessions I had to make to travel to the United States for studies. He believes if people know who I am, it will create problems for him back home and abroad."

"Well, your secret is safe with me."

"I didn't ask you to keep it secret."

For the sake of civility, and because I have to spend the next fourteen hours sitting next to him, I let his comment go.

"Don't think I'm a fan of the metahumans out there today. The majority use the most powerful energy source known to man to pull cats out of trees for adoring children."

"I think they just want to help out wherever they can," I reply

"They're thinking too small. Few, if any, metahumans show an interest in how their powers work. They're content with only knowing only that they work, even though we experienced a worldwide failure of metabands a decade ago. We're no closer to understanding what caused that event, yet those who own metabands today could not care less."

He's not wrong, but I can't tell him I know why the first wave of metabands stopped working.

"So, what do you think should be done?" I ask, genuinely curious about his ideas.

"Whatever the solution is, we can only find it through research. We cannot call these objects magical. They exist in the real world, and while they may defy currently known science, that does not mean they do not follow scientific laws. We simply haven't discovered what they are yet, but I believe we're on the right track."

"What do you mean?"

"Hopefully we'll see when we arrive in Wichita Meadows."

It's starting to click why Midnight wanted me on this trip. Whatever experiments they're conducting in Wichita Meadows, it sounds like they've discovered some aspect of the metabands that the rest of the world, outside Kaldonia, hasn't yet. That's reason enough to investigate.

"So, I understand you and Sarah used to date," Kyle says, snapping my train of thought in half.

"Uh, yeah, for a little while," I say, fighting the urge to ask, *What's it to you?*

Instead of asking anymore questions, Kyle takes out a pair of expensive headphones from his bag, places them over his ears, leans back, and closes his eyes.

I guess that's the end of that conversation. I'm not positive, but this sure feels like some kind of mind game crap, and I refuse to play along—for now. Plus, he already has his headphones on, and they're noise canceling, so I'd have to shout to get his attention.

Okay, so I guess he won this round.

I take out the headphones that came for free with my phone and stick them firmly into my ears. Just as I'm about to try to grab some sleep too, Derrick taps me on the shoulder and wordlessly motions for me to follow him.

I step over a sleeping Kyle and follow Derrick to the back of the bus where I find he has an entire row to himself while I'm stuck next to Kyle.

"What's up, I can only stay back here for a minute. If Muldowney finds me he's going to lose his mind."

"I wanted to talk to you about our, um, mutual friend."

I give him a quizzical look, so he elaborates by putting his hand over the top half of his face.

"Oh, Midni—Middleton," I say in a pathetic attempt to correct my near screw-up.

Derrick glances around. Satisfied no one is eavesdropping on our conversation, he says, "Yeah, Middleton, sure. Are you in the dark as much as I am about all this?"

"I'm not sure how in the dark you are, but if you're totally in the dark, then yes, we're at about the same level."

"Hmm, guess he expects us to play this one by ear."

"We?"

"Hey, from what I understand, you and I are at the same power level." He taps my wrist where my metabands usually are, albeit phase-shifted. "Although I admit I still have a slight advantage thanks to my better looks."

"Because you're old?"

"I'm not old."

"You're older than everyone else on this trip."

"I'm younger than any of the other chaperones. In fact, I think I'm a good twenty years younger than all of them. But

I didn't ask you to come up here to debate who's the better-looking brother."

"What do you want to discuss then?"

"Well, I wanted to see if you knew anything I didn't, but I also wanted to tell you to be careful. Neither Mid—Middleton nor Michelle asked me what I thought before assigning you to this team. I'm glad they arranged for me to tag along, but I'm still not happy with either of them. They both know more than they're letting on. I want you to keep that in mind. Don't take any unnecessary risks. They didn't give you any parameters, so they can't be upset if you return empty-handed."

"There is one thing I've found out that feels relevant," I say. "You know my seatmate, the guy I think is seeing Sarah? Guess who his dad is?"

"Mikah Akulov."

"Wait, how did you know that?"

"I'm not a complete idiot, Connor. Technically, I am a reporter. I did do some *basic* research on the cab ride to the academy. The people at the research facility are no doubt aware of that too. I expect that they'll be watching all us of even more closely as a result."

"Cool. Nothing like adding an extra challenge to my first spy mission."

"You probably won't want to say that out loud again."

"Excellent point."

"I'm going to catch some zs before we get to the hotel. I suggest you do the same."

"Roger that," I say before heading back to my seat, where I'll pretend to sleep for the next roughly thirteen and a half hours.

TWELVE

Kyle wakes me with an unnecessarily hard shove and says, "We're stopping, get up."

Turns out my plan to pretend to sleep lasted all of a minute before I actually fell asleep and stayed asleep through the night.

I didn't realize I was so tired. It makes sense. Between running around the city at night as Omni and getting up early for classes, I haven't had a good night's sleep in weeks. I've been finding it hard to fall asleep anyway. There are always too many things to think about, too many situations to analyze while I lie wide awake in bed.

Jim's snoring doesn't help either.

I rub sleep from my eyes and see that everyone is already standing in the aisle, waiting to exit the bus. Sarah waves in my direction, and I wave back one second before realizing she was actually waving at the person next to me: Kyle.

The trip is already off to a great start.

Eventually we exit the bus and file into a small, outdated bus station. Everything is in shades of beige, brown, and orange. It also looks like we're the only bus here, with no other visible arrivals or departures.

I discreetly position myself out of Muldowney's line of sight.

"All right, everyone, gather up. Chaperones, can we get a quick head count to make sure everyone's here?" Muldowney says.

"Does he think someone jumped out?" I whisper to Jim.

"Excuse me, Mr. Connolly, are you a chaperone?" Muldowney asks.

"Uh, yeah, sorry, I was just trying to get on the Wi-Fi. Does anyone know if there's a password or something?" Derrick answers, still staring at his phone.

The other students all laugh.

"Sorry, I forgot there are two Mr. Connollys on this trip. Who knew one man could be so lucky," Muldowney quips.

The students laugh again, but Derrick has his nose in his phone and doesn't notice. Meanwhile, I've practically turned purple with embarrassment.

A man in a too-large gray suit comes walking toward our group with a large smile underneath his dark mustache.

"Ah, you must be the geniuses from Skyville Academy! My name is Oleg Fresko. Please allow me the honor of formally welcoming you to Wichita Meadows!"

The students and chaperones applaud, and I join in, even though I'm not sure why we're applauding. But I'm pleased with myself for blending in seamlessly like a true spy. Then I catch myself smiling and consciously wipe the smile from my face, still impressed with how great I am as a spy so far.

Muldowney is shaking hands with Oleg. After a brief conversation, Muldowney turns to address us.

"Huddle up, everybody. Mr. Fresko will be our guide

and liaison throughout this trip. Whatever he says goes. I want you to treat him no differently than you would me, except for you, Connolly. I want you to show him more respect than you grant me."

"Got it, no problem," Derrick answers, still only half paying attention.

Muldowney smiles before continuing. "I'm sure I don't have to remind you how privileged we are to be guests here in Wichita Meadows. I want to stress that idea: we are *guests*. If you have any questions about anything, please ask me or Mr. Fresko, and we will be happy to answer them. If you are unsure about anything, *anything* at all, please ask before acting. Your individual actions will reflect on our group as a whole. Keep that in mind. I don't want the actions of one individual ruining the trip for everyone, but those are the terms we've agreed to and must abide by as guests."

"I could not have said it better myself, Mr. Muldowney," Oleg says.

He scans the faces in our small crowd with an ear-to-ear grin. I watch his face as he locks eyes with Kyle. His smile flickers before he quickly averts his gaze. Of course he knows who Kyle is, but I still make a note in my mental spy notebook.

"If you'll all follow me, I'll show you to the shuttle," Oleg says and we begin to walk through the bus station. "I apologize that we have to have you change buses for the remainder of the journey for security reasons. However you'll be pleased to find out you'll be staying at one of the finest hotels we have in the area."

Muldowney stops the entire group in its tracks to make another announcement. "I'd also like to remind you all of cardinal rule numero uno: You are not, and I repeat *not,* to leave the hotel without my or Mr. Fresko's supervision under any circumstances unless I assign you another guide. This is by far the most important rule. Does everybody understand?"

He scans each face one at a time and waits until he gets either a firm nod or a spoken "yes" before we move again.

As we walk, I notice my shoulder bag feels especially light, reminding me I certainly did not pack enough clothes. The group moves forward, and a few students move past me as I slow to peek inside my bag.

"Come on, you're not supposed to dilly-dally," Sarah says.

I look up and notice the rest of the group has pulled a few feet ahead from us.

"*Dilly-dally?* Picking up the local dialect already," I joke.

Sarah doesn't laugh. Instead, she just walks away. I quickly zip up my bag and jog to catch up with her, matching her pace.

"Not everything's a joke, you know, Connor," she says. "Everyone else on the team worked their butts off for months to make this trip happen. If the people at the research facility catch you goofing around, they'll throw everyone back on the next bus home. If you can't take this seriously, the least you can do is not screw it up for everyone else."

Oh, that stings.

"Sorry," I say, swallowing my pride. "I was just checking to see if I forgot anything I might need."

"And the bus station of your destination is the best place to do that?" she asks.

I open my mouth to answer, but realize the question was rhetorical.

"You better not tell me you brought something you shouldn't have," she says in a hushed town. "Namely, two things you shouldn't have."

"Huh? Oh! *Those*. No, of course not. Midnight's hanging on to them for me."

Sarah stops dead in her tracks before hurrying back into motion, realizing falling behind would draw attention to her —literally what she just scolded me for.

"Are you kidding me?" Even though she whispered, her tone tells me she'd have yelled the question if she could.

"No. Why would I kid about that? If there's one person I can trust with them, it's him."

"He put you up to this, didn't he?"

"Nobody put me up to anything. Not really, anyway."

Sarah shakes her head furiously.

"I should have known. How else could you and your brother join this trip at the absolute last minute? It all makes sense now. Glad to see you're prioritizing your schoolwork now."

"What does that mean?" I ask.

"Come on, Connor. We both know you're close to getting booted from the academy because you're too busy doing *you know what* late at night with your roof-hopping pal."

"I know that. I just wasn't aware you knew that. How do you know that?"

"It's obvious to anyone who cares."

"You care?"

"That's not how I meant it."

We're quiet for a few steps.

"Look, it's your life. Get kicked out of the academy if that's what you really want. I just want you to know this trip is important to everyone else, and I don't want your reason for being here to interfere with that."

"I won't be interfering with anything. I'm here to observe, that's all."

"I've heard you make similar claims before."

"Well, I don't know what else to tell you. It's the truth. If you're so mad at me, why are you hanging out back here with me instead of up there with your new BF."

Sarah glares at me with shocked disbelief, and I instantly regret the words that came out of my mouth. She squints at me in a way that reminds me of how I look when I shoot energy blasts with my eyes.

"Not that it's any of your business," Sarah begins, staring straight ahead, "but Kyle isn't my boyfriend. If that's the other reason you're tagging along, then maybe you should get back on a bus and go home."

Before I can apologize, she hurries to catch up with our group.

Great trip so far.

THIRTEEN

At the hotel, Muldowney informs us we'll only be staying there briefly. He gives us enough time to drop off our luggage and tells us to meet back at the bus. He also instructs us to leave our cell phones behind in our rooms since they will not be allowed where we're going next. We're so far from the rest of civilization I don't think anyone's had a signal in hours anyway.

I haven't stayed in many hotels, but something about this one creeps me out. The hotel looks dated, like it was built in the 1970s, but everything appears new. At first, I think they must have built it recently using an older design. Upon further inspection, though, it seems more likely the hotel is old but has barely been used.

The hallway carpeting is beige, the color washed out by time, yet it has no other discernible wear. The same goes for the electrical outlets: The design is outdated, but they look newly installed.

Moreover, the hotel seems empty except for our tour group and a handful of staff. The receptionist and porters all have huge smiles plastered on their faces. Considering the only thing around for miles is Wichita Meadows, it's pretty safe to assume that might be whom the workers at the hotel actually work for.

Jim and I are sharing a room, a welcome relief. We chuck our luggage onto our beds, claiming them, and then head back out toward the lobby with our backpacks. I mention the hotel is giving me the creeps, and Jim replies by holding a finger to his lips. He gestures to the light fixtures in the hallway. He suspects there might be listening devices throughout the hotel.

Almost anywhere else in the world and this would be uncalled for paranoia, but I'm learning there is no such thing as uncalled for paranoia in Wichita Meadows. The government likely won't reprimand us for criticizing the hotel's decor, but keeping our mouths shut is a good habit to get into.

Almost everyone is already gathered in the lobby. Muldowney warned us to come right back after dropping off our luggage, which I think was unnecessary. There isn't much to do or explore at this hotel. Our cell phones don't work, and our rooms don't have TVs. Given the general sense of unease and eerily quiet hallway, heading back to the lobby ASAP must have seemed like a good idea to everybody.

Muldowney does a head count as we march back onto the bus.

"I have a little bit of a surprise, everybody," he begins as the bus gets rolling. "Thanks to some last-minute adjustments by Mr. Fresko, instead of the standard tour we are being given a demonstration of a top-secret project that the scientists at Wichita Meadows have been working on. This is something that no one outside of the facility has ever seen before. This is a once-in-a-lifetime opportunity, and I hope it isn't lost on any of you how significant this is for each of you *and* Skyville Academy. I hope I will not have to explain again how important that is or warn you to remain on your absolute best behavior. Now is not the time to flout the rules you've all agreed to. Your actions represent everyone back home, so let's make sure we do it right."

We pull onto the highway, and it strikes me that we're the only vehicle on the road. The road is bumpy, and the rickety old bus we've been transferred onto doesn't seem to have any suspension. We're bouncing up and down and out of our seats, and the noise from the road makes it hard to have a conversation. Someone taps me on the shoulder. I look up, and Derrick gestures again for me to follow him back to his seat.

"Did you know anything about this?" he asks.

I look around and put a finger to my lips, mimicking Jim's earlier warning.

Derrick looks confused for a second, then yells in my ear, "Trust me, there isn't a microphone on Earth that could pick up our conversation over all of this noise."

"No, I didn't know," I yell back.

Derrick looks thoughtful for a moment, then says, "We have to be careful."

"Why?"

"This is the most secretive place on Earth, but they're inviting a group of high school kids into their main research facility without pretense? It doesn't make any sense."

"Well, we are all very smart."

"No offense, Connor, but it's a high school robotics team. You guys aren't exactly cracking the mystery of cold fusion."

"No offense taken. I couldn't put together a LEGO robot if they asked me to."

"This change in plans might be meant to ferret out anyone who's here with ulterior motives."

"Right," I say, forgetting what *ulterior* means.

"You have that look in your eyes like you're agreeing with me even though you don't understand."

"No, I don't."

Derrick looks at me in disbelief. "Just so we're crystal clear, I think this demonstration is meant to expose the two of us. They're putting out a big tasty piece of cake to see if anyone tries to lick the icing when they think no one is watching. Just remember they're always watching, even if they lead us to believe differently. Don't take any unnecessary risks. We'll have other chances to gather intelligence. Even if we only get to see the interior of the building, then the entire mission has been worthwhile. Understand?"

I nod, tired of yelling over the roar of the bus.

Derrick gestures for me to head back to my seat. I arrive just as the bus pulls off the highway and onto a smoother road. The noise level inside the bus decreases by tenfold.

"Everything okay?" Jim asks.

I nod and look at him like I'm not sure why he's asking, just in case anyone is watching us.

The bus rolls to a screeching halt. Outside the window is a guards' station. Roughly half a dozen guards fan out. Two split up and walk along either side of the bus, holding long-handled mirrors. They sweep the mirrors under the bus, looking for bombs or other suspicious devices.

The door to the bus swings open, and two guards enter. One has a German Shepherd on a short leash.

"Ladies and gentlemen," Muldowney announces, "this is standard procedure for entering a secure facility. Please stay in your seats and open your bags for these gentlemen to inspect. The quicker we can get this out of the way, the sooner we'll be inside, taking a tour of the facility."

I hoist my backpack off the floor and place it on my seat. I glance back at Derrick. He isn't looking at me, but he seems calm and composed. There's no reason for either of us not to be. This search isn't unexpected, and it's precisely why we brought nothing suspicious with us. Anything we report back to Michelle and Midnight will be purely from memory.

I'm still looking over at Derrick when the German Shepherd sticks its snout in my bag, startling me. I instinctively pull back and the dog lunges forward, barking and snapping its jaws. The guard yanks the leash just in time, and the dog's teeth close just inches from my face. He shouts a command in German, and the dog immediately ceases barking and sits by his side.

"S-sorry," I stammer. "I didn't see him there. He surprised me."

The guard merely sticks his hand inside my bag and rummages through it at random. He removes a few items, like my notebooks, and thumbs through them, making sure nothing is sandwiched between the pages. As he searches, I mentally check that I didn't pee my pants.

Satisfied I have nothing illegal on me, the guard moves down the aisle without a word.

Ahead of me, the second guard is rummaging through Sarah's bag. He is asking her questions about the contents of her bag, but Sarah is at a loss for what to say. Muldowney, to his credit, quickly intercepts, explaining to the guard that this is a robotics team and they have brought some of their projects along with them since they are too valuable to leave unattended at the hotel.

"Gentlemen, gentlemen, this is unnecessary," a man

says from the bus's entrance. The man climbs the stairs and stands in the aisle. He is wearing a white lab coat over a dark blue suit. His curly dark hair hangs just below his ears. A pair of round silver wire-rimmed glasses sits on his nose.

The guards stop their inspections and exit the bus.

"I'm sorry for that. These men were following orders, but they have not yet been briefed on who our esteemed guests are today. Please accept my apologies. My name is Dr. Steven Weinheimer. I am the Executive Director of Research at the Wichita Meadows Advanced Testing Facility, and I'm very excited to welcome you all."

The bus door slams shut, and the bus lurches forward down the private road, past the guards' station. The path is winding with dense foliage disguising what's ahead.

"I want to thank Skyville Academy for accepting my invitation to visit. I know we haven't been able to be very forthcoming about what we are about to show you today, but I'm so happy you took a leap of faith.

"Today, it will be my pleasure to show you some of the work we are conducting at the institute, work I hope we will soon share with the rest of the world as we march toward a future where many of today's problems are relics of the past."

Jim makes a subtle gagging gesture, not taken in by the good doctor's flowery speech. There's a second of pure panic as we both glance up to see Dr. Weinheimer staring directly at us. He waits a beat, then takes a seat next to Muldowney. I look back at Jim and give him a mimed *whew* of relief.

After following the winding path for a few more minutes, the bus stops in front of a large slate gray building. The structure is sleek and modern, standing in stark contrast to hotel we're staying in. Multiple levels inside the structure are visible through the large panes of glass, with people in white lab coats strolling from end to end. All the students are in awe at just how large the building is.

Muldowney instructs us to make our way outside and we're then led inside the building. In the lobby, we have to line up to have our pictures taken individually. After a short wait, we're each handed a plastic badge emblazoned with a full color mugshot.

"Cool, a souvenir," Jim says.

"Unfortunately, you must return those at the end of the day," Dr. Weinheimer says, appearing out of nowhere.

"Oh, okay," Jim replies nervously.

It's a good reminder of what Derrick told me earlier: We should assume we're always being watched and listened to.

Once everyone is set with their badges, Dr. Weinheimer and Mr. Muldowney gather us together.

"I want to again remind you all that it is an incredible privilege to tour this facility," Muldowney tells the group. "That means go nowhere you're not supposed to, touch nothing you're not supposed to, and absolutely no photographs. Though I've already warned you to leave your phones back at the hotel." Muldowney stares directly at me. "Let this serve as your second and final warning."

"Now, without further ado, we'll be on our way," Dr. Weinheimer says.

FOURTEEN

The opaque glass doors behind Dr. Weinheimer slide open on cue, revealing a bustling lab. Scientists and computer screens are everywhere. Everyone is deeply involved in their work and barely pays us any attention as we walk through, even though we're among the only outsiders to ever visit.

"Many of you may not have heard of this facility before, and the reason is simple. We need to maintain the utmost security as we work toward our objectives. Every country on Earth would love to get their hands on the innovations we are developing in this laboratory. We need to operate in secrecy to protect our projects, but now we are close to perfecting what has been our primary drive and purpose for a number of years. This creation has taken our facility's entire focus, and we wish to begin sharing it with the world now that we have properly cultivated it."

I glance at Derrick, surprised by what we're hearing. Derrick meets my gaze, and then focuses back on Weinheimer.

"You may wonder why we would share this innovation

with a group of students before anyone else. The reason is simple: We believe this technology is the future. When we fully unveil it, many in the mainstream scientific community will question our discoveries and methods. They will scrutinize us relentlessly. We understand and welcome the scrutiny, but we do not wish to waste time convincing those who do not want to be convinced. Instead we would rather share this with you, the young minds that will go on to shape the future of technology for decades to come."

Weinheimer taps his badge next to another set of sliding glass doors. They slide open, and we follow him into a much smaller and quieter hallway lined with windowless doors. It reminds me of the facility under the academy, except cleaner.

Weinheimer stops at a door, and the group stops with him.

"Take a second to remember this moment. Once we step through these doors, I believe your lives will be split into two time periods: the time before and the time after."

I don't have to look at Jim to know he's subconsciously rolling his eyes.

Weinheimer smiles and taps his security card against the reader next to the door. He then turns to face the reader and removes his glasses so it can scan his retinas. Satisfied they match the records on file, the reader unlocks the door and grants us access.

"Please, follow me," Weinheimer says in hushed tones.

He leads us into a relatively small room. Three scientists in lab coats glance up when we walk in. As soon as they see we're with Weinheimer, they quickly cast their eyes to the floor and scurry from the room.

Once the entire group has squeezed into the room, the door behind us automatically shuts, blocking out all ambient noise. We crowd in around the structure in the room's center. It's a circular table three feet across, covered in what looks like an aluminum dome.

"Do we have everybody?" Weinheimer asks. "I wouldn't want anyone to miss this part."

With the confirmation everyone is present, Weinheimer places his palm on a flat metal plate jutting from the table. A small engine whirs to life, and the aluminum dome retracts into the table piece by piece, revealing the contents within.

On the table is a layer of black sand, but the color is too uniform to be natural. Two students near the front apprehensively lean over the table, checking in with Weinheimer as they do to make sure it's safe. He nods. If Weinheimer is disappointed we're not impressed, he's hiding it well.

"I admit, it appears to be nothing more than a pile of sand, and I wouldn't blame you if you were wondering if I've gone mad, but I assure you I am quite sane."

"Never trust a guy who insists he's sane when you haven't asked," Jim whispers.

There're enough murmurs and side conversations to cover the remark. Everyone is speculating what the stuff is and what it does.

"What you're looking at is a new material we call magtonium. It works quite differently from any other material known to man, but that's not its most important attribute, which is magtonium's ability to generate energy. Even the small amount of magtonium on this table can generate enough energy to power a large city indefinitely."

This claim elicits a handful of chuckles and sighs. Barring myself, the students on this trip are no dummies. They attend the top preparatory academy in the country, and they didn't get in by luck. Most of them plan to study engineering at the top universities around the world. They understand energy. They understand physics. And they understand a table covered in sand cannot power an entire city indefinitely. Even I'm questioning why we're here.

"I understand your reluctance to believe my statement without evidence. However, I ask you this: Hasn't our understanding of physics been rocked to its core over the last two decades? Have metahumans not fundamentally changed everything we thought we knew about the human condition and science?"

Dr. Weinheimer's words hang in the silent room. He's right. Most of us in this room were born after the first wave of metahumans had already begun. We only knew a world without them when they disappeared for a decade. Is it so much harder to believe this table of sand could power a city than to believe that a man or woman can fly?

"How does it work?" a student asks. I don't know his name but he already has a notebook out, eager to learn more.

"I should be clear, magtonium alone is not responsible for this reaction," Dr. Weinheimer says. "There is another ingredient that is necessary."

Dr. Weinheimer turns his back to us and places his palm against the table. A small drawer disengages from underneath and Weinheimer produces a single metaband. He shows it to the group. Students gasp and begin chattering amongst themselves.

Derrick and I exchange glances across the table. I can't tell from his poker face, but I don't think he was expecting this. I certainly wasn't.

"Is that what it looks like?" the same student asks.

"Indeed, it is," Weinheimer answers.

"Where did you get it?" Sarah asks.

The heads in the room all swivel to face her. It's a fair question, but also a loaded one.

"We acquired this metaband through a private collector."

"You know many of the metabands that come from private collectors are stolen, right?" Sarah pushes.

It's quiet enough to hear a pin drop. This is the exact type of question we were told to avoid.

"We are aware of that, which is why we follow a stringent process to ensure the metabands we acquire were not procured through unseemly methods," Weinheimer says with a broad smile.

Despite his politeness, it's obvious he won't tolerate this line of questioning much longer. It's pointless anyway since Weinheimer is almost certainly lying. These are surely questions he was prepared for one of us to ask. Still, if Sarah keeps pushing him, I worry he'll wrap up the tour before it's over.

I casually tap Sarah's elbow to get her attention, hoping to warn her to tread more lightly. Instead of it being discreet, though, Sarah whips her entire head around to face me.

"What?" she demands.

I was wrong about how quiet it was before. Now you can *really* hear a pin drop.

"Sorry, you had, um, some dust on you," I stammer.

Sarah glares at me and faces away again.

I doubt that could have gone any worse.

"If you'd like, I can give you a demonstration of the technology?" Dr. Weinheimer says, breaking the tension.

He takes the metaband in both hands and carefully places it in the middle of the magtonium-covered table. Satisfied with its position, he pulls his hands back and waits.

For a few long seconds, nothing happens, and I wonder if this is all some elaborate fraud.

Then, something happens.

It's hard to see at first, but slowly, almost one by one, grains of magtonium cling to the sides of the metaband and work their way up, covering the surface. The layers of magtonium grow thicker and thicker until they completely coat the outer and inner edges of the metaband.

There are surprised gasps. Some of the braver students lean forward to observe the effect more closely. Then I notice the magtonium itself is changing. Where it was once uniformly black, there are now small flecks of red. The flecks are glowing, almost pulsating, but I can't tell if that's what I'm actually seeing or if that's how they look compared to the infinite blackness of the material.

Then the most impressive part begins. The metaband slowly sinks into the table. The red flecks multiply and connect, forming a network along the surface of the sinking metaband. The red lines glow in unison, and the speed at which the metaband is sinking into the table increases until it disappears.

A student ducks his head under the table.

"It's not there."

Dr. Weinheimer chuckles. "No, it wouldn't be."

The magtonium is again flat across the table, but small pieces of it are glowing like molten lava and seem alive.

"If anyone is interested, you may touch the magtonium," Weinheimer says.

The student who ducked under the table reaches out and places his hand on the table.

"It's cold," he says in astonishment.

"And safe," Weinheimer says. "What you have witnessed is a process we are days away from announcing to the rest of the world. In fact, you've served as somewhat of a test audience to gauge your reaction."

"And what exactly did we just witness?" Sarah asks.

"Nothing short of a miracle. And like all true miracles, this one results from science."

"But that stuff just ate through a metaband," Derrick says. "That's impossible. Metabands are the hardest material known to man. There are only a handful of instances of them even being damaged, but those cases involved other metaband-enhanced factors."

Great, now he's asking questions too. Why can't everyone just wait and see what he tells us instead of making themselves marks? For the record, I'm doing a fantastic job of pretending to be too stupid to ask questions. It's working out well for me.

"It didn't so much *eat through* the metaband as it merged with it," Weinheimer says. "The metaband and the magtonium have combined at the subatomic level, meaning they are impossible to separate. However, magtonium is a far more malleable material than the substance that comprise metabands. This allows us to extract the energy contained within them."

"So they're just fuel now?" Derrick asks.

"Not exactly, but you're close. The reaction you witnessed brought the metaband's energy to the surface, where we can extract it through other proprietary methods."

"Will you be showing us those methods as well?" Derrick asks.

"I'm afraid they aren't terribly exciting, certainly not as thrilling as watching the two substances merge. From here, there are a series of processes to extract the energy in a safe and efficient way. It does not differ from the energy produced through methods such as burning fossil fuel or harnessing solar energy. The difference is that the amount of energy we can extract is an order of magnitude larger than any other method, including nuclear. Unfortunately, as we have seen this week, there are many inherent dangers with nuclear power that do not exist with magtonium."

Derrick pulls a small notepad from his back pocket and begins scribbling.

"How do you know this is safe?" Derrick asks.

"We have done extensive research and testing. One thing we can tell the world with certainty is this energy source is infinitely safer than trusting metabands with individuals who may use them for their own dark purposes."

"You're talking about metahumans?"

"Yes, of course. The world can't even agree on how many metahumans exist, let alone how many have people have died because of their actions. The most conservative estimate of the death toll remains in the tens of thousands, though. Why are we allowing this? Because, unfortunately, once Pandora's box is open, there is no way to close it again. We offer an alternative, a means to use what we found after we, as a society, opened that box and didn't like what we found inside. What if instead of allowing a single man to topple over a skyscraper, we use these objects to further humanity in a meaningful way?

"If even half of those who hold metabands gave them up for the greater good, we could solve humanity's energy crisis within a generation. Concerns about manmade climate change and pollution would cease to exist. Wars over energy reserves would stop if clean, free energy were available to everyone in the world. Imagine the leaps in technology that might be possible and the ideas we could dream up if such a miraculous invention were made globally available?"

"So you plan to open-source this technology?" Derrick asks.

"In time, yes. For now, we are concerned with showing our work to the world at large. We believe once enough metahumans have laid eyes on what is possible, the decision will be simple for many, if not all."

The room is quiet as everyone takes in what Weinheimer has said. The government doesn't exactly have a reputation as trustworthy, for no other reason than its constant secrecy, but it's hard to argue against the idea of free global energy.

"It's a lot to take in, I know, and I'm sure many of you are exhausted after your bus ride from Skyville. There will be plenty of time this afternoon to answer your questions and provide more insight into how we accomplished what the rest of the world assumed was impossible. And I have not forgotten about your exciting projects. In fact, we are hoping to work with you later to see where we might use magtonium to power your creations."

This gets a few people excited, at least the ones who aren't shell-shocked by what they've seen and learned.

"Now, if you'll follow me, I'll lead you to our cafeteria where we have a fabulous lunch waiting for you. We want you all full of energy this afternoon. We have a lot more in store for you."

FIFTEEN

After the magtonium demonstration, the rest of the day moves by swiftly. I find it hard to pay attention to anything else they show us since it all pales in comparison. I'm alone in feeling this way. The other students—i.e. the ones who deserve to be on this trip—are having a blast learning about all the different robotics technology they're developing at Wichita Meadows.

I remain a quiet observer while the other students pepper the scientists with questions or show them the projects they've been working on, hoping to get feedback.

Derrick disappears to conduct a private interview with Dr. Weinheimer.

At the end of the day, the chaperones shepherd us back onto the bus, and we travel back to the hotel. Dinner is waiting for us in the hotel's otherwise desolate restaurant. I'm hoping to catch up with Derrick and find out what he's learned, but he tells me he has to skip dinner to get a head start on editing the Weinheimer interview.

I wind up eating alone. I could have sat with Jim, but that would have meant sitting with a bunch of students who are mad I made it onto this trip. Everything they talk about goes over my head anyway.

After dinner, the chaperones send us upstairs for an early lights out, but not before Muldowney warns us against leaving our rooms. We're boarding the bus back home bright and early, and he doesn't want to have to knock on any doors.

"Where were you?" Jim asks as we trudge upstairs to our room.

"I ate by myself."

"Why?"

"Just seemed easier."

"You're not having a great time, are you?"

"Not really. I didn't understand ninety-nine percent of the stuff they showed us. The one percent I did understand was about a new material that can literally eat the two most valuable objects I own."

"I hadn't really thought about it that way."

We reach our room, and Jim uses his key to open the door. I flop down on the bed as Jim pulls his laptop out of his bag.

"You find a Wi-Fi signal?" I ask.

"Nah, I wish. I just want to type up some notes I took."

A few minutes later, I'm literally staring at the ceiling. All I can hear is Jim typing on his laptop from the twin bed next to mine.

I'm dangerously bored.

"Hey, do you think you can get a cell signal from the roof?" I ask.

"Um, I don't know. It is the tallest building around, so maybe? Why?"

"I'm thinking about trying it."

"Did you not hear Muldowney tell us to stay in our rooms?"

"I did, but I want to tell Midnight what we saw today."

"You can't wait until tomorrow?"

"This is a big deal. If he knew they were working on magtonium here, he'd have told us before we left."

"I could rattle off a dozen things he didn't tell you about until after you figured it out yourself."

"Okay, even better. If he already knows about magtonium, I want to learn more about it."

"And you can wait until tomorrow."

"True, but I'm bored now."

Jim sighs. "Look, if you want to sneak out onto the roof, I won't stop you, but if Muldowney catches you, I'm telling him I was already asleep when you left."

"Fine by me."

I jump up from my bed, excited to finally have something spy-like to do.

"How do you plan on getting up there?" Jim asks.

"Jim, please. If there's one thing I've gotten good at over the past few months, it's figuring out how to get onto rooftops undetected. This place is so ancient it doesn't even have security cameras. This will be a piece of cake."

IT ISN'T a piece of cake. Not only do I almost run into Muldowney, but I also almost set off the smoke detector while trying to short-circuit the emergency exit alarm. After a few minutes and a minor electrical burn, I make it onto the rooftop undetected.

It's dark up here, and I can barely see my hand in front

of my face. The hotel is way off the beaten path, making it almost impossible to get a cell phone signal.

I wake up my phone and hold it high in front of my face, fishing for a signal.

Nothing.

With the phone held overhead, I slowly walk toward the far end of the roof to see if the reception is any better.

"It won't work," a voice says from the darkness.

I jump and almost fumble my phone. Squinting into the darkness, I glimpse the red glow of a cigarette. The person holding it approaches until we're close enough to see each other's faces.

"I tried it too," Kyle says.

"Oh, damn. I thought the roof might be high enough to grab a signal," I say, trying to play it cool even though he'd scared the crap out of me.

"Want one?" he asks, holding out his pack of cigarettes.

"No thanks."

"Wow, so you just came up here to make a call? You must be more addicted to that thing than I am to these."

I laugh like he'd caught me red-handed. Better for me that he thinks I'm up here for a social media fix.

"Where's your buddy, Jim?" he asks.

"He's downstairs in our room, sleeping," I lie, remembering my deal with Jim.

"Probably a good idea. You've known him for a long time?"

"Not that long."

"Huh. I would have thought you guys knew each other your entire lives considering how well you get along."

"It feels that way sometimes. We've had our share of disagreements, but we've stayed pretty tight."

"He seems like a good guy. He reminds me of the best friend I used to have."

"Used to?"

"He died."

"Oh, I'm sorry. I didn't mean to—"

"It's okay," he interrupts. "It was a long time ago." Kyle takes a long drag of his cigarette. "His name was Demetri. He was the son of one of the housekeepers we had. At the time, my father was still just a general in the army. Demetri would come to work with his mother, and we would spend the day running around outside, pretending to be metahumans. His family was very poor, but as a boy, I didn't understand that. All I knew was that he was my friend, and I didn't care that we lived in different worlds. I didn't realize just how different our worlds were until he died."

"I'm so sorry to hear that. I lost people close to me when I was young. It's hard."

I don't tell him those people were my parents. I'm sympathetic, but I'm not willing to be that vulnerable in front of him.

Kyle pulls on his cigarette again. He holds the smoke in his lungs for a few seconds before loudly exhaling and saying, "He was killed by a metahuman."

"Excuse me?" Caught off guard, I'm not sure I heard him correctly.

"A metahuman killed him."

"Didn't you say it was a long time ago?"

"Yes, it was during the first wave. Right before the end of it, actually. A metahuman crashed into the tenement building Demetri and his family lived in, causing it to collapse. Three hundred and seventeen people died."

"Oh, man."

Kyle nods.

"It was one of the worst disasters in my country's history, but the president refused to do anything about it. The people were furious at his cowardice. My father took advantage and launched a coup. After he became president, he banned all metahumans from Kaldonia. The people loved him for it."

"Why have I never heard about this?"

"A week later, the infamous battle occurred in Empire City, overshadowing our tragedy, and the world moved on. But my father didn't. Convinced they would return one day, he remained obsessed with keeping metahumans out of Kaldonia. He turned out to be correct."

Kyle's dad predicted what few others had.

"He poured the nation's resources into preparing for the metahumans' return and purchased plans for a device from a scientist who had been involved in an anti-metahuman cult. The scientist claimed the device could deactivate metahumans at close range. My father kept the plans locked away until the second wave of metahumans appeared. Imagine our surprise when the device worked. Its only drawback is the amount of energy it requires. We solved that problem when we discovered magtonium."

"I don't understand. You're saying Kaldonia discovered magtonium?"

Kyle throws his cigarette to the ground and stomps it out.

"Yes. We've known about it for some time. Kaldonia is the only place on Earth where magtonium can be found."

"How does Wichita Meadows have it then?"

"They stole it, obviously. We are a very poor country. Things are different there. Scientists and officials can be bought off. I'm sure the government here would not hesitate to stoop to theft, especially for a reward as valuable as magtonium."

"Wow, I had no idea. Not that I doubt what you're saying. Most governments would do anything to get their hands on something like that."

"Wichita Meadows acts like they've discovered it themselves, though they have to have stolen it from Kaldonia. It makes me furious to think about." Kyle grows quiet and presses his lips into a thin line. "We should go inside before someone catches us out here."

As I follow him toward the rooftop exit, curiosity gets the better of me, and I ask, "Whatever happened to the metahuman?"

"What metahuman?"

"The one that caused the building collapse. Did Kaldonia ever bring him to justice?"

"No. He died a week later when he threw Jones into the sun."

SIXTEEN

I couldn't sleep at all last night. All I could think about is what Kyle told me. Could it really be true? Could my dad have caused that kind of destruction and simply left it all behind? I can't imagine him doing that, but I never knew him as The Governor, only as my father. It sounds like it was an accident, but that doesn't excuse not taking responsibility for his actions. None of this makes any sense. Derrick might know the truth, but I'm afraid to even ask right now.

The bus ride back is loud. Everyone is talking about what Weinheimer showed us and how it will change history. Some speculate using magtonium on a large scale will significantly reduce the number of metahumans around the world. To my displeasure, many seem fine with this sacrifice. I have to bite my tongue to not join in the argument. I'm a metahuman, after all, and my parents were both metahumans. I haven't been one for long, but my life has changed so much I can't imagine going back to a time without my metabands.

But maybe I'm being selfish. Maybe Weinheimer is right. On the whole, metahumans might be doing more harm than good. For every new metahuman who saves cats stuck in trees, three more pop up who are only interested in robbing banks or causing mayhem. Is that really worth sacrificing free energy for the entire world?

I keep all this to myself for fear of being outed. Luckily, I'm sitting next to Jim, who is also keeping his mouth shut. I'm dying to talk this over with Derrick too, but I can't. Not until we get back home.

There's suddenly a loud pop and the bus shudders. Smoke begins pouring out of the hood. There are gasps and shouts.

"All right, just calm down everyone," Muldowney announces.

He rises from his seat to face the back to the bus but finds he has trouble maintaining his balance, bracing himself with both hands against the back of a seat.

"I gotta pull over," the driver says over his shoulder.

The bus slowly rolls to a stop, the black smoke still billowing from the hood. The driver engages the parking brake and opens the door to step outside and investigate the cause of the engine trouble.

We're under a thick canopy of trees, deep in the forest. We've been on the road for a few hours now and I can't remember the last time I saw any signs of civilization. A quick check of my cell phone confirms we're still in the middle of nowhere without a cell signal in sight.

The driver emerges back through the door and beckons Muldowney to come speak with him outside. Everyone watches the conversation through the bus windows but it's impossible to hear what's being said. Muldowney is shaking his head and looking down at the ground. The driver shrugs his shoulders and heads back to the hood of the bus while Muldowney climbs back inside.

"Does anyone have a cell phone that is able to get a signal?" He asks.

I briefly consider retorting *I thought we weren't allowed to use our cell phones until we're back home?* But Muldowney looks stressed enough, and I can't imagine that comment going over well right now. The other students pull their cell phones out to check, but there are a chorus of noes. Muldowney grunts in frustration.

"I have a satellite phone," Derrick announces from the back of the bus.

Of course he does.

Muldowney breathes a sigh of relief.

"Thank goodness. We've got some engine trouble the driver says he can't fix so we're going to need to call for a tow."

"Sure, but my phone needs line of sight in order to connect. It's not going to work with all these trees covering the sky, but I can go hike up that hill and see if I can find a clearing."

"Fantastic."

"I'll come too," I say.

"That's fine, in fact why don't we all stretch our legs for a minute. We might be here for a while," Muldowney responds.

The students and chaperones file off the bus along with Derrick and myself.

"Let's head this way," Derrick suggests, pointing toward a path that leads uphill.

"It's your sat phone, so you're the boss."

I follow Derrick as we begin up the path. Once we're outside of earshot from the rest of the group I start asking him questions.

"So what did you learn from Weinheimer?"

"Not a whole lot, unfortunately. He refused to answer questions about where the magtonium came from or how they discovered its truly unique properties."

"Kyle told me last night it's from Kaldonia."

"When did you talk to Kyle?"

"I may have snuck out for a little bit."

"Connor."

"Hey, it was worth it if I got some actual new information. This is supposed to be a spy mission, remember?"

"Did he tell you anything else?"

The story of the apartment complex collapse flashes into my mind, but I dismiss it. I don't want to deal with thinking about that right now.

"No, that was it. I'm not sure how much he knew about it."

The path splits, and we take the trail that leads to higher ground.

"You're remembering which way we came so we can find our way back, right?" I ask.

"Sure, we just head downhill."

"You're not exactly inspiring confidence."

"Look, up ahead."

The path becomes steeper, but at the end of it a blue sky is visible through the canopy of leaves.

"That should work," Derrick says.

We have to grab onto saplings along the side of the path as we trek uphill. At the end of the path, the ground levels out and we find ourselves in a small clearing.

"Perfect," Derrick says as he pulls the satellite phone from his bag.

He punches a few keys on its screen and puts it up to his ear. A smile on his face tells me it's ringing. He speaks with a tow truck company on the other end of the line and gives them the last mile marker we spotted before thanking them and hanging up.

"No problem, they'll be here in an hour."

"And we're just stuck in the woods until then?"

"Unless you're aware of another tow truck company closer by that you'd like to call."

I can't remember even seeing another car on the road in the past hour let alone a tow truck company.

Leaves rustle nearby.

"Do you hear that?" I ask.

Derrick perks his ear up and nods.

"Are there bears here?" Derrick asks.

"I'm pretty sure there are," I say.

"And you didn't think that was relevant information to share before we went trekking off alone into the woods?"

"I thought you knew, you're the chaperone."

"Hey," a voice says from over the edge of the steep incline we just climbed. It's no bear though, just Jim. Sarah is following him closely behind, carrying her backpack.

"Oh, thank goodness," Derrick says, bending over and holding his stomach.

"Uh, what's your problem?" Jim asks.

"He thought you were bears."

"There aren't any bears in this area," Sarah says.

"Yeah, that's what I said too, but Derrick wasn't convinced," I lie.

"Were you able to call a tow company?" Jim asks.

"Yeah, they're going to be here in about an hour."

"That's not good," Sarah says.

"I said that too, but it's apparently the closest one around."

"There's something weird going on," Sarah begins, "the driver found the cause of the problems. It wasn't the engine;

it was the axles. He climbed underneath for a look, and they are completely covered in a tangle of vines. They're wrapped so tightly they caused the engine to overheat."

"What? I've never heard of anything like that," Derrick says.

"The driver hadn't either. He was a little freaked out."

"What could cause something like that?" I ask.

"No idea, but it's extremely strange. Muldowney wants to get us out of here as quickly as possible."

SEVENTEEN

Derrick and I follow Jim and Sarah back down the path. They seemed to have done a much better job remembering the way back down than us. With the woods being so dense with foliage, it's difficult to tell how close we are until we're practically on top of the bus.

"Sounds like we're almost there," I say.

"Who is that talking?" Sarah asks.

We're still too far away to see the bus through the trees, but we can hear a voice shouting.

"Is that Muldowney?" Derrick asks.

"No way," I respond, "I'd recognize his shouting voice."

"Then who else would be yelling?" Jim asks.

It's a good question, and one that tells me we should be cautious. I still don't understand what exactly happened to the bus, but all of this is very suspicious. I slow my pace and motion to the others they should do the same. The floor of the forest is covered in dry leaves and branches that will give away our approach if we aren't careful. If we're quiet, we should have a good idea of what's going on before we make our presence known.

Jim finds a large log off the beaten path and motions for us to come to him. He's knelt down, peering through the trees. He points to show us where he's looking so we can join.

Through the branches, the bus is visible on the roadway, but there aren't any students.

I reposition to find a better angle. Now I can see the other students and chaperones.

They're all lined up single file with their hands resting on their heads. Standing across from them are a pair of men holding automatic rifles. They're not pointed at them, but they are ready to be at a moment's notice.

It seems impossible, but the forest seems to have closed in on the scene. The limbs of trees are stretched across the roadway, blocking the path in or out.

Pacing between the two groups is a strange looking man. He was hard to spot initially since he blends in with the forest as though he's wearing camouflage. But as I look closer, it's obvious that it's not camouflage he's wearing. He's actually covered in tree bark with small twigs and leaves sprouting from his head.

Around his wrists are two metabands.

I glance over at Derrick who shrugs his shoulders.

This must be a new one for him too.

"You're not going to tell me, huh?" The tree-like man says.

He has a thick accent I cannot place immediately.

There's no response from the crowd.

"They are bad people, you know this correct? Mikah Akulov and his people have beaten, tortured, and killed innocent men and women. Do you know what he does with the metahumans who are brought to him? He uses them to generate energy to further his own personal wealth. Day in and day out, metahumans are confined to primitive machines to harness their powers. They are like medieval torture devices. Hamster wheels where they are forced to run to create cheap electricity. Hydraulic pistons that they must push over and over, thousands of times per day. They cannot leave. Their families are told that they are dead.

That is what they have told me about my sister. But I know this cannot be. I can feel that she is still alive. And once I have the son of Mikah Akulov to barter with, I'll be able to prove it. So, I ask you once again, reveal yourself and your classmates will be let go. Choose to stay anonymous and there will be consequences."

"Can you get them to me?" I whisper to Jim.

"Huh?"

"Can you get them to me? The metabands."

Jim's eyes bulge out of his head.

"I know Midnight must have something that can get them here," I say.

"What, like a missile? Come on, Connor, you know there're limits to what he can access."

"I should have never let him convince me to leave them behind."

Derrick waves to grab our attention and motions for us to slowly follow him back up the path. Jim, Sarah, and I do, all while being careful to generate as little noise as possible. Once we're a safe distance, Derrick begins to speak.

"We're going to need some assistance here and I don't think we have much time. I'm going back up the hill to call for help. Michelle will be able to send someone who can reach us before they're able to hurt anyone or take Kyle."

"Ah, so Kyle is the name he has taken, is it?"

A previously unseen soldier emerges from the forest. He's holding a handgun at hip level, pointed at all of us.

Crap, this just made everything a lot more difficult.

We all instinctively raise our hands to show we're unarmed.

The man holding the gun is dressed in what looks like an old Kaldonian army uniform that has seen better days. The edges are all frayed, and it looks like it could use a dry cleaning. I wonder how long they'd been waiting in the forest to ambush us.

He reaches for a walkie-talkie on his belt and brings it up to his face. He softly speaks a few Kaldonian words into it. A few seconds later another soldier emerges from the trees from further up the hill. They must have suspected we were out here and sent a search party to round us up.

The newly arrived soldier zip-ties my hands behind my back, then does the same to Sarah, Jim, and Derrick.

"You won't get away with this, you know," I say.

Before I can register what's happening, there's a white flash of light and intense pain bursts in the back of my head. The ground flies up, but my hands are zip-tied behind my back. My face hits the ground nose first. Tears fill my eyes, and I wonder if my nose is broken. I turn onto my side to pull my face out of the dirt. The world comes back into focus, and I see the first soldier standing over me, the butt of his handgun aimed in my direction. It's what he must have hit me with.

Derrick and Jim scream at them to stop. They're swearing and threatening them. The other soldier laughs. The one who hit me reaches down, laughing in my face. He grabs a fistful of hair and pulls me onto my knees.

Still dazed, I notice Sarah isn't screaming like Derrick and Jim. Her face is red with rage, and her eyes are locked on the soldier who assaulted me. He notices her and laughs even harder. He gestures to the soldier and points to her.

When he sees the anger on her face, he can't hold back his laughter.

Sarah's gaze shifts.

Through the soldiers' laughter and Derrick's and Jim's shouting, I hear her say two words: "Screw this."

She pulls her hands in front of her from behind her back. The soldier nearest her notices she's out of her restraints and panics, but the next part starts before he can raise the alarm.

Sarah grabs her bulky backpack straps and pulls down hard. The backpack responds as you would expect—the straps tighten and the bag rises higher on her back. After that, though, things take a left turn.

In a matter of seconds that pass in slow motion, the backpack takes on a life of its own. Steel plates emerge from the top, locking in place over her shoulders. From those pieces, more interlocking plates telescope down each arm. At her hands, the plates break off into smaller pieces to cover her fingers.

More armor emerges from the sides of the backpack and wraps tightly around her torso. Once the torso pieces are locked in place, individual parts ricochet down each leg to her feet, covering them in white metal.

From the neckpiece, a final series of plates click into place over her face. The holes over her eyes glow white.

It's Midnight's suit. Sarah not only kept it, but miniaturized it and made it portable. If that doesn't get her a letter of recommendation for college from the robotics club, I don't know what will.

One of the soldiers places his hand on her shoulder to stop her, but he's too late. Sarah's exoskeleton-covered hand grabs the soldier's hand and grips it tightly. The soldier cries out in pain, and then Sarah flings him into a tree.

The remaining soldier fumbles to raise his firearm. As he does, a projectile shoots out of Sarah's suit. It hits its target, and the soldier is asleep before he hits the ground.

With a flick of her hand, Sarah slices through my zip-tie restraints. She then does the same for Derrick and Jim.

Sarah raises a hand to her helmeted head and depresses an unseen button. The mask collapses to reveal her face.

"Thanks for waiting until the last second to disclose your science project," I say.

"I figured I ought to do something if Omni wasn't showing up," Sarah retorts.

Ouch.

"I have to stop them before they figure out who Kyle is. You wait here. I'll be right back," she says.

The pieces of her mask fall down her face like magnetic dominos. She crouches, and a series of hydraulic pistons hidden within the suit compress. Assisted by the tech in her suit, she leaps and launches almost a hundred feet into the air, back toward the road. In the distance I hear the faint sound of metal hitting pavement as she lands.

"What do we do now?" I ask Derrick and Jim.

Derrick is holding his phone high in the air as it boots back up, trying to grab a signal from the satellite. It connects and emits a loud beep. He looks at the display and breathes a sigh of relief.

"I've got confirmation of delivery," he says.

"Huh?"

"I sent an emergency S.O.S. with a location beacon. It means Michelle knows we're in trouble and help is on the way."

"And in the meantime? Sarah is down there taking on a metahuman and his soldiers all by herself. We have to do something to help her," I say as I start down the path back to the roadway.

Behind us, there's a loud thud.

The three of us turn at once to find Sarah, still in her mech suit, kneeling beside the tree-like metahuman. He appears to be unconscious.

I rush over to Sarah. "Are you okay?"

The suit is beeping loudly and various lights are blinking red.

"Help me with this," she says.

From a compartment in the arm of her suit she extracts a compact pair of metahuman restraints. I take the handcuff-like device and clamp the locks around the metabands on the metahuman's wrists.

Safely secured, Sarah presses a button on her belt. The suit retracts all at once, tidily folding itself like a gigantic metallic piece of origami, back into her backpack.

"Thanks, my fingers were too big with the suit on to press the little buttons on that thing," she says.

"You took those guys on all by yourself? You were gone for like 15 seconds," Jim says in disbelief.

"He can control plants. You thought he was going to be able to go toe-to-toe against mechanized titanium battle armor?" Sarah asks.

"No, I guess not."

"Were you able to call for help?"

"There should be a team inbound to pick up Treeman any minute," Derrick responds.

"Great, we should get back down there then. Don't want anyone figuring out my secret identity," Sarah says in a flat monotone. The comment is clearly aimed directly at me.

She doesn't wait for agreement from the rest of us before she begins hiking back down the trail.

When we arrive back at the bus, the trees blocking the roadway have retracted. The metahuman's accomplices have all been tried up using bungie cords, which I recognize from the bus's luggage area. None of them seem to be in any shape to put up a fight even if they weren't restrained.

There's a buzz in the air as the students and chaperones are all excitedly recalling the brief skirmish between Sarah and the Kaldonian metahuman. It sounds like it happened so quickly some of them barely even got a glimpse of her.

"No, it was all white. I don't know if it was a suit or a robot or what. All I know is that it was in and out of here like a ghost."

Sarah glances back at me and smiles, "Ghost, huh? I kinda like the sound of that."

Kyle rushes over to Sarah and gives her a hug.

"I was worried something had happened to you," he says.

"I'm fine, I'm glad you're okay too," Sarah responds.

"Thank you for keeping my secret," Kyle says, exchanging a look with me as well.

"Um, no problem," I reply.

"I owe you, and I won't soon forget it."

EIGHTEEN

"Why on earth did you think bringing a portable mech suit on a field trip to a top-secret government facility would be a good idea?" Midnight asks Sarah.

We had only been back at the academy a few moments before me, Jim, and Sarah received a message from Midnight demanding we meet with him in the underground facility immediately.

We were all in trouble.

He hands me my metabands without breaking eye contact with Sarah. I put them on and concentrate to shift them out of our reality. It feels good to have them back, and I can already feel a decrease in the swelling on my head from where the soldier hit me with the butt of his gun thanks to the residual healing properties of the inactive metabands.

"Because it was a good idea," Sarah replies. "If I hadn't, who knows what might have happened."

"I had other contingencies in place."

"Well, thanks for telling us about them."

"You weren't a part of this operation."

"No, I wasn't. I was actually *supposed* to be there, Connor wasn't. Thanks for risking the entire trip without asking anyone who'd worked hard to make it happen if they were okay with that, by the way."

"Maybe it was a mistake letting you keep my suit."

"This is unbelievable. You almost ruined *my* trip, and I saved the day with *my* suit, but somehow this is all my fault? And it is *my* suit now. After the alterations I've made, it's almost unrecognizable."

"It's kinda true," Jim interjects. "She figured out how to fit it into a backpack. Like, a regular backpack. It was insane when she activated it, and suddenly…"

Jim notices Midnight's glare and realizes Midnight isn't interested in geeking out about Sarah's new suit.

"Right, I can tell you about that later."

"Tell me what you saw," Midnight says, changing the subject.

"A lot and not much," I explain. "They're working on something called *magtonium*. They claim it will solve the world's energy problem forever. The only catch, and it's not really a catch for them, is that it runs on metabands."

"Explain."

"I'm not sure I can. They brought us into a room where they had a bunch of the stuff on a table—"

"Describe the stuff."

"Uh, it's black. Kinda looks like sand. Didn't look like anything special *until* Dr. Weinheimer dropped a metaband into it."

"Then what happened?"

"It swallowed it. It's like it absorbed the metaband. After that, the magtonium looked a little different. It had these little red specks inside it that glowed."

"And how does it generate energy from there?"

"No idea. They didn't explain that part. But it swallowed a metaband. I've never seen anything like it before."

"That's concerning. You're certain it was a real metaband?"

"Pretty sure. I know there are good fakes out there, but I can usually tell the difference. There's a type of sheen I've never seen replicated. The way the magtonium interacted with it was completely unique."

"Did they explain how they created the substance?"

"Nope. They said they developed it in their lab, but Kyle said it was stolen from Kaldonia. That would explain how they're able to produce so much energy, although the Treeman who tried to kidnap Kyle told us it's all a lie and they're actually generating energy using enslaved metahumans."

"The notion a cash-starved country like Kaldonia could build a world-class laboratory and create a world-changing substance like what you're describing doesn't add up."

"What does that mean?"

"It means I remain dubious of their claim that magtonium can produce usable energy, and I am almost certain they didn't create it."

"Who did then?"

"I'm not sure. It would be easier to figure that out if I had a sample to analyze."

"Yeah, sorry about that. I think they would have noticed if anyone tried to pocket a handful."

"That's fine. The operation required you to maintain your covers, which you did—mostly." Midnight glances at Sarah.

"So, what now?" I ask.

"For now, continue, or in your case Sarah, *begin,* lying

low. Despite the near-disastrous turn the trip took, I consider it to be a success overall."

"We didn't even bring anything back."

"You brought back knowledge we didn't have before. Both Kaldonia and now the United States government possess a substance that can destroy metabands. Even if their claims about its creation and energy-producing potential are lies, that is still significant. I need to do more work to place its origin and hopefully track down a sample for further study. In the meantime, you all need to avoid unnecessary attention. Got it?"

NINETEEN

I wake up unaware of where I am, what day it is, the time, anything. Panic starts to set in before I remember I'm home, or rather in my dorm room and it's Saturday.

The past few days have fully caught up with me, and a glance at the desk clock confirms I've slept in late.

Looks like Jim is already out for the day. The dork even made his bed. I guess serious and focused Jim is better than anti-metahuman gang Jim, but that doesn't mean I still can't give him crap about his tidiness later.

I consider closing my eyes and drifting back to sleep until dinnertime. I have a literal mountain of homework to finish, but other than that, I don't have much to do today. Maybe a lazy day would do me good.

Instead, as has become my habit, I roll over onto my side and grab my phone off the end table. I squint before I wake it up, afraid of what notifications might be waiting for me. Usually, if I sleep in this long, I wake up to find I've slept through some unmitigated disaster. Either that or there's a litany of increasingly angry messages from people like

Midnight or Michelle, informing me I'm supposed to be training somewhere.

Luckily, I don't have any notifications, but I also don't have a message from Sarah. I had kinda hoped she'd message me after our experience in Wichita Meadows.

I swipe over and open a messaging app to send her a text message asking how she's doing, but I hesitate. This is exactly what made her so angry at me in the first place. We're not together anymore, and I don't have a right to know where she is every hour of the day.

Looking to avoid a potentially negative situation, I start lazily scrolling through different apps on my phone, hoping to distract myself. I switch to a news app and see there are no mentions of what happened in Wichita Meadows. Looks like everyone managed to keep their mouths shut like they were told. Wichita Meadows isn't even supposed to exist, so news about a metahuman looking to kidnap a foreign leader's son returning from a field trip there is exactly the type of attention they're looking to avoid.

The phone dings with a new message.

An unexpected rush of nervousness hits me before I read the message. Part of me wonders if it's Sarah telling me never to talk to her again and leave her alone. I take a deep breath and open the app.

Hello. This is Kyle. Do you have a few minutes today? If so, can you come to my place later? The address is 39 Sycamore Place. Apartment 406.

IT TAKES me a while to find Kyle's apartment. It's ridiculous that someone my age has their own apartment. I thought I was lucky to have the freedom of living in a dorm room, but that was before I found out how bad Jim's socks smell.

Turns out that students living in off-campus apartments isn't all that rare. Ironically, every billionaire in Bay View City started sending their kids to Skyville because of its reputation as a meta-free institution. I shouldn't complain, though. Their tuition offsets everyone else's. Plus, Derrick had to go and get all rich, so it's not like I can judge anymore.

Between thoughts of how awesome it must be to have your own apartment, I think about why Kyle invited me here. Maybe he likes Sarah and wants my advice on how to pursue her. The thought makes my stomach turn. "You can't like Sarah because I still like Sarah" is what I *want* to tell him, but that'd go over like a lead balloon.

Then my dumb brain jumps to an even more horrifying idea: He wants to talk because he's *already* dating Sarah. Sarah told me they were just friends, but maybe she wasn't being completely truthful? She could have been lying to protect my feelings. That would suck, but I'd understand. No one knows what to say in such situations, and they often jump to the answer that will cause the fewest problems in the short term.

I probably would have done the same.

But then my brain takes a monumental leap to the worst possible reason he invited me over: He's dating Sarah, knows I have feelings for her, and wants me to stay away from her. In that case, I really don't know what I'll do or say. It seems ridiculous, but who knows? Kyle's family is immensely wealthy. He's probably used to always getting what he wants. Would he treat a relationship any differently?

As usual, I'm so lost in my thoughts I almost miss a turn.

Then I practically do a double take. Sarah is walking toward me.

Ugh. My worst fears are coming true. She's here because *they* want to talk to me together. This is a literal nightmare.

"Are you straight up following me now?" Sarah asks.

"What? No," I say.

"Seems like you are. What are you doing way out here then?"

"I'm here to see Kyle."

"You are?"

"Yeah, I assumed you knew about this."

"Knew about what?"

"Why Kyle wants to talk with me."

"Kyle wants to talk with you?" Her shoulders relax when she realizes I'm not here to pick a fight with her possible new boyfriend.

"Yeah." I pull out my phone and show her his text. "I assumed he already told you what he wants to talk about."

"No, I have no idea. I forgot something on the bus home last night and he grabbed it for me. "

"Oh. Okay then," I say, confused and running through other possible scenarios why he wants to see me. "He doesn't know that was you in the mech suit, right?"

"No. At least, I don't think so."

"You don't think so?"

"If he thinks it was me, he hasn't said anything. If anything, he probably thinks it was you since no one knows how you got on the list for the trip."

Behind Sarah, I see Kyle approaching us. He's jogging with something in his hand. When he sees I've noticed him, he waves and slows down. Sarah turns to see what caught my attention.

"Hey, there you are," he says.

Kyle hands Sarah her denim jacket. She looks down sheepishly.

"I'd forget my head if it wasn't sewn on," she says. "Thank you, Kyle."

"Hey, Connor, on your way to my place?"

"Um, yeah."

"Cool, great."

"Why is Connor coming to see you anyway?" Sarah asks.

I'd like to know the answer too, but before I can say anything, Kyle confidently jumps in.

"Tutoring."

I start to open my mouth, but Kyle subtly winks at me, and I decide to see where he's going with this.

"Oh, Connor said you texted him to come over but didn't say why," Sarah says as though I'm not standing right next to them.

"He's probably embarrassed, but like I keep telling him there's no shame in needing help. The only shame is in pretending you don't."

"Aw, well, that's very nice of you," Sarah says.

"Yup, it sure is," I say sarcastically.

They continue to treat me as if I'm invisible—an ability I didn't have even when my powers were working correctly.

"Well, I'll let you get to it. Good luck, guys, and thanks again for grabbing my stuff, Kyle. I owe you one." Sarah turns around and walks away, leaving me with Kyle.

This is somehow even more embarrassing than I'd imagined.

TWENTY

"Sorry about that. Had to come up with an excuse on the fly," Kyle says as we enter his apartment building. He presses the up button on the elevator. The door opens and we enter.

In the silence inside the elevator, I feel like I'm about to burst out of my skin. Why has he invited me here? The anticipation is killing me, so I turn to Kyle to break the silence.

"Hey..." I begin uneasily.

"Just wait. We'll be at my apartment in a few seconds."

This is getting stranger and stranger.

The doors open onto Kyle's floor.

"I'm right over here," he says.

He opens the door to Apartment 406 and enters.

"You don't lock your door?" I ask, looking for something to say to fill the silence.

"A retinal scanner is embedded in the lock. It verifies my identity as I approach and unlocks the door for me."

I'm impressed. Even in our state-of-the-art facility we

still have to put our faces right up to the scanners to unlock certain doors. I wonder if Kyle is more paranoid than Michelle and Midnight, or if he's just a rich kid who likes to spend his money.

Inside the apartment, it's obvious it's the latter. The ceilings stretch high, and every corner is furnished with a gadget I don't recognize. A wraparound TV screen that's gotta be twice my size sits above a glass fireplace in the living room. The kitchen is stainless steel and glass throughout. Even the refrigerator has an all-glass front, which I didn't even know existed, not like I'm a kitchen technology expert or anything.

"That stuff is cool," Kyle says, noticing me taking it all in, "but the really cool stuff is this way."

He motions for me to follow him down the hall to a plain door. I'm surprised that he once again has to verify his identity, this time through a retinal scan I'm more familiar with.

"This one requires registration the old-fashioned way, but it's harder to trick," he explains.

What kind of room needs a more secure lock than the one on the front door? I'm sensing Kyle has a few secrets, and this visit is more about those than Sarah. Surprisingly, this relaxes me. I deal with secretive weirdos every day. I'll take secretive weirdos over having to talk about my feelings for Sarah any day of the week.

I follow Kyle into the room and notice a stark contrast between it and the rest of the apartment. It feels dark and claustrophobic. There aren't any windows, and the walls are painted black. There are desks along the far wall topped with several computers. In a corner, there's a large server rack, its noisy fans humming away.

Kyle moves to a steel cabinet on the far side of the room and pulls a sliding keyboard from a hidden gap in the side.

"Welcome to my workshop," he says with a smile on his face. "Bet you haven't seen many places like it."

Between the training facility and Midnight's various home bases, I reckon I've seen roughly half a dozen like it.

"I wanted to show you something I've been working on. Obviously, you know robotics is one of my passions."

Kyle finishes typing, and the cabinet unlocks with a hiss. Whatever the cabinet contains must be under some type of pressure or climate control. He pushes the keyboard back into its slot and opens the drawer. Carefully, he removes a small metal box and carries it to the center of the room.

"Can you move that table over?" Kyle asks, gesturing to an unusually tall round table.

I do as he asks. He opens the box and removes a small black circular disk, which he places on the tabletop.

"I know it isn't much to look at, but the disc holds a few secrets," he says.

Kyle stares at me, smiling, and waits for my reaction.

"What am I looking at exactly?" I finally say.

"Of course. I'm so focused on my work it doesn't always occur to me not everyone will understand it."

How am I supposed to be impressed when he hasn't even told me what the hell it is?

"This will change everything."

"Uh, is it a DVD or something?"

Kyle laughs so hard and loud it startles me.

"Funny. Very funny. Sarah said you were a funny guy."

Cool, real glad to hear those guys talked about me outside of my presence too.

"I never noticed that before, but it does indeed resemble

a DVD. However, the technology is far, far beyond that. Perhaps you will recognize it in its natural state."

Kyle picks up a tablet and taps a few commands onto the screen. After a brief delay, the black disk disintegrates into a pile of sand-like material.

It's magtonium.

TWENTY-ONE

"Wait, what?" I ask. "Is that what I think it is?"

Kyle simply smiles and nods.

"Are you serious? Is this from Wichita Meadows?"

Kyle's smile fades. "Where I acquired the magtonium is not what's important here."

"How could it not be important whether it was stolen from a secure government facility or not?"

"This magtonium was not stolen. It, like all magtonium, belongs to my father and was presented to me as a gift. However, due to... disagreements between Kaldonia and America, smuggling it into the country was the only way I could continue my research. Unfortunately, we have had issues with moles inside our research facilities. This is likely how Wichita Meadows acquired their magtonium in the first place. It is why my father granted me permission to continue working independently."

"That didn't answer my question."

"I'm sorry, perhaps I've made a mistake. I thought we had gotten to know each other over the past few days, and I genuinely appreciated you keeping my secret when I know that had to have been difficult. There aren't many people here I can trust."

Kyle taps a button on his tablet and the magtonium solidifies back into a disk. He then picks up the disk from the table, places it back into its box, and returns it to its drawer.

Now I'm the one taking deep breaths. With seemingly everyone in the world being mad at me right now the last thing I want to be involved with is knowing the location of presumably stolen government property. Still, it's in my best interest to let it go if I want to learn more about what Kyle's up to.

"It's fine. I get it."

Kyle pauses and turns back without closing the drawer.

"You do?" He asks.

"Yeah, I do. It's complicated. You've got to do what you've got to do sometimes. That's science, right?"

Kyle smiles. "Thank you, Connor. I truly appreciate it."

"So, you were going to show me what your magtonium can do?"

His smile widens, and he retrieves the disk and places it on the table again. Another tap on his tablet returns it to its sand-like form.

"There is a secret to magtonium Dr. Weinheimer did not disclose during the tour. This secret allows magtonium to behave in the unusual way it does. You see, each grain might look like sand, but they're actually tiny machines."

I give him a puzzled look and then lean closer to inspect it.

"I'm afraid you can't see the inner workings of the machines with the naked eye. The machines are actually nanotechnology. Each is impossibly complex and capable of feats of engineering many scientists think are impossible in modern physics."

"Seriously?"

"The scientific community thinks of Kaldonia as a backward nation with few resources to offer the rest of the world. They could not be more incorrect. Not only are we the only place on Earth with the necessary material to build this technology, but we also understand how to use it in ways that the US government has not even dreamt of. But perhaps a demonstration would be best."

Suddenly, the sand jumps to life and rearranges itself from a scattered mess strewn across a table into a solid cube. When I glance back at Kyle to confirm what I'm seeing is real, he chuckles and taps another button on the tablet. I turn and see the cube has already rearranged itself into a perfect sphere.

"How...?"

"How did it do that? I can communicate with the material through the software I've written. Each piece is perfectly in tune with its surrounding pieces, allowing them to reconfigure themselves in any way I'd like almost instantaneously."

"Can I touch it?"

"Of course."

I tentatively brush my fingers over the surface of the sphere. Though I just saw it arrange itself out of sand, the surface feels mirror smooth.

"You don't have to worry about being gentle," Kyle says.

"It isn't fragile? Even with all the... machines or whatever inside it?"

"Nope. That's one of the many unique properties of magtonium. It's practically indestructible."

Confident Kyle won't throw me out of his apartment if I

break something, I put my entire hand around the sphere and squeeze. It feels like solid steel with no give whatsoever.

"Perhaps you would like another demonstration of how magtonium charges itself?" Kyle asks.

It's posed as a question, but he doesn't wait for my response. The magtonium on the table shifts back to a pile of sand-like particles.

Kyle places the tablet on the desk and retrieves a small black velvet bag from another drawer in the cabinet. He grins as he approaches the table. Standing next to me, he pulls out a familiar object from the bag.

I don't even have to ask. I can tell by sight it's a real metaband.

Kyle places the metaband onto the pile of magtonium, and we watch as it consumes the metaband, pulling it into itself. Tiny grains that were once black take on an electric shade of red.

He retrieves his tablet and taps a few buttons. The magtonium transforms. Not into a solid object this time, but into an amorphous blob that writhes and pulsates on the table. Within a few seconds, the blob takes on a less liquid form and looks more like a giant upright jellybean that's sitting on the table facing me.

"Move," Kyle says.

"Oh, I didn't realize I was in the way."

"You're not in the way. Just move."

"Um, where?"

"Anywhere."

I take a small step to my right. The blob pivots to follow me. I glance at Kyle and then take a larger step to my right. Again, the blob tracks my movement. I take a few more steps back and forth, and each time the blob turns to face me.

"Try touching it again," Kyle suggests.

I hesitate.

"Don't worry, it will do nothing to you," Kyle reassures me.

I again reach to touch the object, but just as my fingertips reach it, the shape changes to avoid my touch. I pull my hand back and try again, but again the magtonium pulls away.

I try to catch it off guard by quickly reaching for it, but the magtonium is too smart and again dodges my hand.

Kyle is laughing with joy.

"That's the artificial intelligence I created at work. Instead of taking commands from a remote computer, my AI is uploaded directly into the magtonium's memory, allowing it to adapt on the fly. My programming directed it to avoid being touched but did not specify how to accomplish that goal. It figured out a way to do it all on its own."

"Wow," I say.

I'm already thinking about all the people I want to tell about this: Michelle, Derrick, Midnight. They won't believe this is what magtonium is actually capable of.

"You're the only person I've shown this to so far."

"This is amazing, but why show me first? We barely even know each other."

"You may not know much about me, but I know an awful lot about you, Omni."

TWENTY-TWO

"I don't know what you're talking about."

I say this, but I don't hear the sounds coming from my mouth. All I can hear is my heartbeat thudding in my red-hot ears.

It always occurred to me that one day someone might figure out I'm Omni. I just never saw it happening like this. Now I'm regretting never thinking through how I would respond.

"Come on, Connor. You don't have to play dumb. It's insulting to both of us. I could have figured it out by myself based on a dozen different inconsistencies, like despite your awful GPA, the academy hasn't expelled you."

"Seriously, Kyle. Is everything okay? You're acting kinda funny. And how would you know what my GPA is?" I ask, hoping he's bluffing, but I know he's not.

"Connor. I'm the son of Mikah Akulov, the president of Kaldonia. We may be small, but even the smallest country has access to vast resources. These are the resources I used to have you followed to confirm my suspicion. I can show you photographs of you with your metabands on your wrists if that will help move this along."

"You had me followed? You can't just have people followed! I have rights."

"All of my research was completely legal. I don't wish you any harm, Connor. Quite the opposite. I need your help. I want to join you."

"What?"

"I want to join you. I am confident that, given enough power, the magtonium artificial intelligence will enable me to harness the same powers as a metahuman, but on an exponentially larger scale. I could do everything you can, and more, without relying on technology we don't understand or fully have under our control."

"Most metahumans have their powers completely under control. There are a few bad apples, but they police themselves to take care of those who don't obey the law when necessary."

"Do they? Because it was a metahuman who could not control his powers who killed my friend and hundreds of others in my country," Kyle says, almost yelling.

Kyle runs his hands through his hair then takes a few steps away from me, needing to reset. He takes a deep breath before facing me again.

"I want to be out there. I want to help. I want to be the hero I prayed would have swooped in at the last minute to help my friend. The hero who never came."

"Even if I were who you think I am, which I'm not, I don't understand how turning sand into a box puts you on the same level as a metahuman," I say.

"Ah, so you'd like another demonstration before you decide whether to help me? Of course. I would ask for the same before I agreed to anything."

"That's not what I meant, Kyle."

It's too late, though. Kyle is already furiously tapping away on his tablet.

"I'll be the first to admit that everything isn't quite working at the level I expected it to, but that's one pitfall of working with artificial intelligence. Like with our own brains, there are few shortcuts to learning. It takes time and trial and error."

"I still don't really understand what artificial intelligence has to do with making this stuff move on its own."

"AI has everything to do with it. The demonstrations illustrate how I can direct the substance to follow a few simple commands. The microscopic machines work independently and co-dependently with each other. They are capable of rapid communication between each other, as well as individual and collective problem solving. That's where their true power lies. Here we go."

Kyle taps a final button on his tablet, and the substance springs to life as though it was struggling to keep its shape this entire time. Within the table's boundary, it moves and flows independently, rising and falling into the air. It spreads to cover the entire surface of the table, and then condenses back into the size of a baseball only to do it all over again.

"What is it doing?" I ask, slightly fearful of it.

There's something about the way it's moving that feels entirely unnatural. A primitive part of my brain is screaming "danger," just like the brain of a caveman would if he saw a snake moving for the first time.

"It's learning. The AI model I uploaded is brand new, and right now, it's being overloaded with input stimulation. It has no information or knowledge of its own, so it is trying to learn as much as it can about its surroundings. It has been seeded with my own neural patterns. In time, it will allow us to communicate with each other instantaneously. It will learn what I've learned and vice versa."

"Is that safe?"

Kyle ignores the question, and I get the feeling his change in personality might be somehow connected to these experimentations.

The substance slows and is no longer flailing wildly. Instead, it pulsates at the speed of a living creature. An offshoot grows out of its body and stretches toward Kyle's face.

"See, it's learning. It just noticed you and I differ from it and the other objects in the room. To artificial intelligence, we're by far the most interesting things in the room because it can learn from us the most."

The substance directs its attention at Kyle's mouth as he talks.

"That's right. I'm the one who programmed you and gave you life," he says to the magtonium. "My name is Kyle."

Kyle stares at the substance, smiling contentedly.

I officially feel weird watching him talk to this sentient goo that looked like regular sand a few minutes ago.

"I think I'm going to get out of here. Sorry I couldn't help you with whatever it is you need."

My attempt to leave snaps Kyle out of his stupor.

"So I'll take that as a refusal to help me, Omni? There's so much the magtonium could learn from someone like you if you would just allow it."

"I'm not Omni, Kyle."

"Then you don't mind if I tell others who you are?"

He doesn't pose this as a question; it's a clear threat.

"It's a free country. You can tell people whatever you

want. Just don't be surprised if they look at you like you've got three heads."

"I assume you intended that as an insult against Kaldonia."

"No, it's just an expression we use here."

"It's true we have some restrictions Americans might find distasteful, but these restrictions allow us to be free in ways other countries can't even begin to understand. You will understand that better as the world learns of our technological advancements. Breakthroughs like magtonium will reshape the world in ways not even a metahuman could dream of.

"I know this is a lot for you to take in, Omni. I understand if you wish to take time to think about it. When you come around, you know where to find me. For now, though, I must return to my work. I trust you remember the way out."

As Kyle spoke, his eyes never wandered from the magtonium. He reaches out to touch it. At first, the magtonium seems scared of him. It flinches away from his touch, then realizes Kyle won't hurt it. He places a hand on it and strokes it. The magtonium responds by rising higher off the table and pushing against Kyle's hand.

He is completely entranced by it, like prey hypnotized by a snake.

I leave without Kyle noticing.

TWENTY-THREE

Monday morning, I'm back in Muldowney's homeroom, waiting for the bell so he can take attendance. We're back to our usual routines. Homeland Security instructed us that if anyone asks the trip was good but uneventful, and we barely left the hotel. But mostly no one asks since the details of the trip were a secret even before we ran into a metahuman.

"Connolly."

"Here," I say, snapping out of my daze to answer the call for attendance. I look up from my desk at Muldowney. He looks like he missed a spot or two shaving this morning. There are dark circles under his eyes. He looks away from me and down at the next name on his paper.

There are only two more minutes until homeroom is over, so I take advantage of it by pulling my hoodie up and resting my head on my folded arms, hoping to catch a glorious 120 seconds of sleep. I've barely shifted into a more comfortable position when a strange feeling comes over me.

I lift my head, and in a panic, yank down the sleeves of my hoodie. My metabands are somehow visible around my wrists without my consciously summoning them. I glance around to see if anyone has noticed, but they haven't.

With my metabands securely hidden under my hoodie sleeves, I close my eyes and concentrate on shifting them out of reality like I have hundreds of times before. But when I open my eyes and pull up my sleeves, they're still there. There's something else odd about them, a sensation, almost like they're warm. I glide my fingers across the left band's surface, expecting to feel the same sensation, but I don't. They feel the same as they always have.

"Everything all right, Mr. Connolly?" Muldowney asks.

I practically jump out of my seat and blurt, overdoing it by 100 percent, "Yup, yes, absolutely. Everything is fine. A-okay."

Muldowney gives me a strange look and then continues taking attendance.

I've never had them not respond before. My worst fears about my metabands going haywire and then losing their powers are coming true, and it's horrifying.

"Connolly, come up here for a minute," Muldowney says.

He's done taking attendance, and the rest of the students are talking amongst themselves, so I avoid getting an "ooh" from anyone. I stand and awkwardly fidget with my shirtsleeves as I approach Muldowney's desk. When I get closer, I can see just how bad a shape he's in. Besides the scruff along his jaw, it looks like his shirt hasn't been ironed. He might have been told not to talk about the events in Wichita Meadows, but it's obvious he spent the weekend thinking about them.

"Do you have last week's assignment for me?" he asks.

Oh crap. I completely forgot.

"Um, let me see if it's in my backpack," I say, desperately buying time to think.

"You're not sure if it's in your backpack? Did you actually complete the assignment, Mr. Connolly?"

"Oh yeah, definitely."

"So, you completed the assignment, which is already a week late, but after the many hours it took to complete, you can't remember if you took an extra five seconds to place it into your backpack?"

"If you want me to be honest, I was up late finishing it, so I may have forgotten to pack it away."

"It's not in your backpack, is it, Mr. Connolly?"

"I'm not sure, that's why I have to check."

He's not falling for this one bit.

"Mr. Connolly, if you did not complete the assignment, please do not waste our time by pretending to search for it inside your backpack, only to come up empty-handed precisely when the bell rings for class, allowing you to put it off for another day."

"I might have it, but if I don't, I can absolutely get it to you tomorrow."

There's something happening. Not inside the classroom but outside. I've encountered enough weird things over the last few months that I'm starting to get a sixth sense for weirdness. It's almost unperceivable at first—a change in the air or background noise. Something. Maybe I can only perceive it because my metabands, though technically inactive, are around my wrists, giving me an early warning.

"I'm too tired to do this today, Mr. Connolly. You don't seem interested in my class or in math. If you do not hand in your assignment within the next thirty seconds, I am marking it as incomplete, and you will receive a zero for the grade."

The sky is darkening. It was happening slowly at first, but now it's like there's a solar eclipse. Other students are noticing it too and moving to the windows for a closer look.

"I promise I can get it to you tomorrow."

"I suggest you do, Mr. Connolly. There is a test on Friday and the homework assignment serves as a measure of how prepared, or unprepared, you are for it, but please remember you will still receive an incomplete, regardless."

"Okay."

My ears pop as the air pressure changes in the room.

"I think it's time we had a frank conversation about your performance in this class. Attending the academy is a privilege, one that is directly tied to your academic performance. If you are not interested in learning, there's little the academy can offer you. I think it's time you gave that some serious thought. As it stands, neither you nor the school is benefitting from the current arrangement.

"Are you listening to me, Mr. Connolly? I'm telling you you're in danger of expulsion if you do not get your act together and complete the work as I assign you, but somehow, you still find whatever is happening outside to be more important than your future here. I don't understand it."

"Sorry," I mumble.

Then Mr. Muldowney notices I'm not the only one staring out the window. Every student is out of their seat and pressed up against the windows. Muldowney turns to look out the window too.

Outside it's nearly black. The only light source is the lightning flashing in the distance, which provides brief glimpses of what is happening. One student rushes over to the light switch and flips it off to clear the glare from the glass and give us all a clearer view. Rain pelts the windows, a few drops at first, then a downpour.

I step away from the crowd and make my way to the empty side of the classroom, still keeping an eye on what's happening outside. I take my wireless earpiece out of my pocket and tap the side to connect with Michelle.

"Are you seeing this?" I whisper so no one else in the room can hear me. They're not paying attention anyway, and the sound of approaching thunder masks my voice.

"I'm watching it too," Michelle responds. "Satellite imagery suggests it's contained to our area."

"Which I'm guessing means it's not natural."

"That's a safe assumption based on the small area being affected and the severity of the storm."

"So it's a metahuman."

"That's our best guess. Connor, whatever you're thinking about doing, don't."

TWENTY-FOUR

Lightning flashes in the distance to reveal a tornado. The other students see it too, and a few begin to panic.

"A tornado's heading this way, Michelle. I can't stand by and watch it rip the school apart. I have to do something. The person responsible must be nearby if they're using their powers like this."

"I repeat, Connor, do not engage. The agreement not to use your powers on campus was meant for such situations. You're too much of a liability right now to pop up at the academy again. We don't know what attention it might attract."

I hesitate. If Kyle already knows who I am, then others are likely close to figuring out the truth too, and having Omni show up at Skyville Academy again will only confirm their suspicions.

"We have another metahuman on their way, Connor. I know this is hard, but you have to stand down until we get this resolved. You can't take on every problem yourself."

The classroom windows all explode. Shards of glass fly

across the room. I put my hands up in time to protect my face, but others aren't so lucky.

The girl next to me, Heather, has blood streaming from a small but deep gash in her forehead. I take the jacket off the back of my chair and rip off one sleeve. Heather stays calm as I wrap it around her head to stop the bleeding.

"Everyone into the hallway!" Muldowney shouts.

Chaos is unleashed as students push past one another to exit the room. Strong gusts of wind pour in through the broken windows, whipping papers and personal items into the air. I help a few students off the ground and guide them toward the door.

"Con—"

A burst of static interrupts Michelle, then the connection goes dead.

I rush to the broken windows and look out.

Outside is dark. It reminds me of when, in third grade, we watched a solar eclipse through cardboard paper towel rolls. Wind and rain smack into my face, forcing me to squint, but I spot a human-shaped silhouette high in the air.

The metahuman is too far away to identify, but it's what's underneath them that's the real danger anyway. The tornado is writhing back and forth like a viper and appears to be growing.

"Omni. Show yourself, you coward," the unknown metahuman shouts. His booming voice is somehow audible over the tornado roaring like a freight train.

To hell with this.

My enrollment at the academy isn't worth putting lives in danger.

I flick my wrists out, metabands at the ready, and bring them together to activate.

Nothing happens.

I try again, bringing my wrists together even harder. Still, nothing.

Crap.

I examine the metabands. They appear dull, like all life has been drained from them. They've been acting strange for a while, but now they're not acting at all.

I cast my eyes back to the sky. The metahuman controlling the tornado is much closer now. He catches my gaze and stares back. I can see he's smiling.

"Ah, there you are," he says. "Prepare yourself to face the wrath of Terrornado!"

Terrornado?

Seriously?

There's no time to question his unfortunate taste in alter ego names, not if I want to survive this. I consider running for the relative safety of the hallway, but what about the other students hiding there? This jerk obviously wants me, and I doubt he'll let a bunch of innocent civilians stand in his way.

There's only one other way out of the room, and that's through the broken window. I can't climb through it with all the jagged glass around the edges.

With no other choice, I take three steps back, pause to collect my nerves, and then charge full speed ahead.

I manage not to hesitate while doing something as stupid as jumping headfirst out of a second-story window. All the flying around must have dulled my fear of heights.

I clear most of the broken glass, but my jeans get ripped up. With that out of the way, I focus on the next part: not breaking my neck on the landing.

Below is a large green bush. I let momentum flip me over onto my back for a soft landing—or as soft of a landing as I can get.

The branches of the bush snap and scrape against my skin as they slow my descent. Now that I've stopped falling, I have another problem: getting out of this shrub. I grasp branches, pull myself upright, and fight through the leaves and twigs to get my feet back on solid ground.

The wind is deafening and getting stronger. I keep low among the trees and bushes that line the school's exterior, but Terrornado must have seen me jump. He'll know where I am.

Between the wind and darkness, I can only see a few feet in front of me. Using the school's brick wall as a guide, I reach out and hurry to get as far away from my landing spot as possible.

Above me, the powerful winds are tearing off the roof's shingles.

The only chance I have of surviving this without working metabands is to reach the training facility. The underground bunker is guarded against natural and unnatural phenomena alike. I tap the communicator in my ear to reach Michelle, but it's no use.

This Terrornado guy won't stop until he's found me or another metahuman takes him down. With Michelle out of contact, there's no telling how far away help is. I try my metabands again, but they're still not working.

Without my powers, hiding is my only option.

At the building's corner, I consider my next move. Michelle once told me about an emergency bunker entrance in the next building over. Disguised as a locker on the third floor, it's essentially an incredibly long chute to the underground training facility. A scan of my handprint should let me inside. All students and staff have likely moved to lower floors by now, meaning I can use the entrance without anyone spotting me.

First, I have to reach it without getting sucked up into a tornado.

I tilt my head skyward and scan the darkness for Terrornado. I see no sign of him, except for the terrifyingly huge tornado he's created with his mind.

Rounding the corner will mean leaving the shrubs' cover, but I won't get a better opportunity.

Time to move.

I run for it and make it roughly ten feet before rain hits me. Then the rain turns into hail. Hailstones the size of marbles hit the ground in front of me; within seconds they grow to the size of golf balls.

One the size of a baseball hits me square in the back, and I tumble forward into the mud. More hailstones bounce off my back and legs as I struggle to stand. I've barely made it upright when a hailstone the size of a grapefruit hits me in the thigh, and I fall to my knees before landing face first in the mud again.

Had it hit me in the head, I don't think I would have survived.

All around, growing hailstones ping off the ground. I need to keep moving, but my leg feels like it's broken. It doesn't want to move. I struggle onto my back, keeping my arms up to protect my face from the onslaught.

Terrornado is looming over me, high in the air. He's laughing. His hands are at his sides, pointed at the tornado below. This must be how he's controlling it.

"The great and mighty Omni, taken down by a ball of frozen water. It's kinda pathetic, don't you think? Don't worry. Whenever a do-gooder meta dies in an embarrassing way, it's usually covered up so no one will know they died like a coward. I'm sure your brother will leave out the humiliating details when he eulogizes you."

Terrornado raises his hands high over his head, and the tornado spins faster and faster until it becomes a gray and brown blur. This feels like the end, but I, again, bring my metabands together to try for activation.

Without warning, Terrornado falls from the sky. His limp body tumbles through the air and crashes to the ground.

The tornado slows, and the hail ceases. All the debris thrown into the air rains down around me.

On the ground, Terrornado regains consciousness and looks up at the sky. His mouth trembles as he tries to speak, but only a trickle of blood escapes. His eyes lose focus, and his head slumps.

The remnants of the tornado vanish, and the clouds part, letting through a sliver of sunlight.

In that sunlight, I spot the person who saved my life. Whoever it is, is hovering in the air in a uniform that looks like mine, except it's black and doesn't have an insignia on the chest. Throughout the black suit are small patches of pulsating red.

The uniform moves as though it's alive, immediately reminding me of the magtonium Kyle showed me.

Without saying a word, the figure swoops down, grabs Terrornado's unconscious body, and disappears into the parting storm clouds.

TWENTY-FIVE

There's a lot of confusion in the aftermath of Terrornado's attack and defeat. Muldowney rounds up all his students to make sure everyone is accounted for. We've run through drills for situations like this and know where to meet up, both inside and outside the school, in case of a metahuman-related emergency.

Ambulances arrive shortly after the sky has cleared. No one is seriously injured, but the paramedics treat a few students for cuts and scrapes. My leg feels better too, making me optimistic that my metabands might be slowly coming back online.

"Are you all right, Connor?" Muldowney asks.

"Yeah, I'm fine. You?"

"A little shaken up, but that's been par for the course lately."

I offer him an understanding smile, knowing more about what he's been through than he realizes.

"That... person back there, the one controlling the tornado, do you know him?" Muldowney asks.

"No, of course not. Why do you ask?"

"It seemed like he knew you, or like he was targeting you."

After the evacuation, no one was close enough to hear the few words Terrornado spoke to me, but at least a few like Muldowney must have noticed he'd singled me out.

"I think he came after me because I was the only one outside."

Muldowney nods thoughtfully. "How did you get outside, by the way?"

Crap.

"Um, I'm not really sure, to be honest," I say, desperately stalling to think of something better. "I must have gotten sucked out of the window."

"But the rise in air pressure knocked the windows in, not out. I don't understand how it could have pulled you out."

Great, my math teacher apparently minored in physics.

"You'd know better than me, I guess. I'm just glad everyone's okay," I say.

Muldowney agrees, and he leaves to check on a few students being treated by the EMTs at the ambulances.

A few satellite trucks are making their way up the road toward the campus entrance. Even without any fatalities, this will be a big news story since it happened at a school. Once the media finds out the strange details about the person who took down Terrornado, they'll be even more interested.

I step away from the crowd and discreetly tap my in-ear communicator, but all I get back is static. Terrornado's weather control must still be affecting the atmosphere and causing this interference.

I'm close to the entrance to the training facility I was trying to reach before the hailstorm took me out. With all the activity around the ambulances and the arriving TV cameras creating a distraction, now's a good time to slip back inside.

I check over my shoulder to make sure no one is watching, or worse following, me as I go inside the building. I find the stairs and hustle up to the third floor. I don't come across any students or faculty, and the hallways appear empty.

After locating the locker, I glance up and down the hallway, and then press my palm to its surface. It snaps open, and I step inside. The ride down is brief since I'm practically free falling. This is an emergency entrance, after all, so the person using it will usually be in a hurry: speed over comfort.

At the bottom, I find myself alone in another empty hallway. I consider heading south to Michelle's office, but think better of it. A few things are bothering me about the Terrornado situation, and the longer I wait to get to the bottom of it, the harder it'll be to find any real answers. So instead of finding Michelle, I check my metabands again.

While they don't look normal, their distinct shine is back. It gives me hope, so I figure it's worth a shot. I bring the bands together, fully expecting them to give me problems. To my astonishment, they work in an instant. I'm Omni again, suit and all.

That's strange.

Why didn't they work when I really needed them?

I'll have to figure that out later. Right now my primary concern is finding out what happened to Terrornado and if the person who took him down was who I think it was.

Down the hall I enter a room known as the Evacuation Chamber. It contains a series of doors with small placards. Behind each door is a tunnel, usually a very long one. The placards provide a brief description of where each doorway leads. The tunnels are only meant to be used to evacuate the facility as quickly as possible.

That hasn't happened yet, knock on wood, but today, these tunnels offer another useful purpose: getting me off campus without anyone noticing.

A placard lists one tunnel's destination as *Evans Lake*, the large lake located in the woods north of campus. I activate the bio-authentication panel and unlock the door.

As expected, it opens to an extremely long tunnel lit by fluorescent overhead lights fifty yards apart.

I will myself into the air and fly down the tunnel. The door automatically slams shut behind me as I increase my speed. The overhead lights zip by rhythmically before I reach a brightly illuminated sign that warns, *Point of No Return*.

I speed past it, and a large wall rises behind me to seal off the tunnel. Then the tunnel begins to fill with water. The water is colder than I expected, but the metabands sense this and raise the temperature of my suit.

The tunnel takes an abrupt 90-degree turn straight up, and I break through the surface of the lake at high speed. No one's around to see my exit, which is a little unfortunate because it must have looked pretty cool.

I've got bigger things to worry about.

I get my bearings and head toward Bay View City. More specifically, I head for the Silver Island metahuman detention center. The small island is still undergoing restoration, but I'm not heading there to see how the rebuilding is coming along. I'm heading there to visit an old friend.

TWENTY-SIX

"Well, well, well," Halpern says as I swoop down from the sky.

Conveniently, he's outside supervising the new construction and has spotted me long before I spotted him. My status at Silver Island isn't sterling considering I had a hand in demolishing the place. I wasn't sure how I was going to get past the front doors without him.

I set down in front of him, and he extends his hand to shake mine.

"You're not mad at me?" I ask.

"Oh, I'm still pissed off at you. Super pissed off. You destroyed my workplace and put a lot of lives at risk. But everything worked out for the best. Mostly."

"I'm sorry about that, if it means anything."

"Not really, but I've been doing this for a long time, kid, and I've learned not to hold grudges. You're one of the good guys. If you could have done more to mitigate the damage, you would have."

"That's a relief. So my privileges are reinstated?"

"Absolutely not."

"Oh."

"Sorry. Those decisions are above my pay grade. Also, you didn't do yourself any favors with the business in Asana either."

"Don't remind me."

"I didn't think I'd need to. Anyway, that means if you've got anyone for intake, you'll have to find somewhere else to drop them off. It's temporary, I hope, until everything blows over."

He's referring to prisoner intake. Back when I was on good terms with Halpern and The Agency, I could bring any misbehaving metahumans to Silver Island. My landing privileges were promptly revoked when I destroyed the place a few weeks ago, even though it totally wasn't my fault. Okay, it was like half my fault.

"I don't have anyone for intake today, sorry."

"I didn't think you did, unless you were keeping a micro in your pocket."

There aren't many micros out in the wild. Like most metaband-provided powers, the ability to shrink isn't very useful without some level of invulnerability. Without it, a lot micros find themselves stuck to the bottom of someone's shoe.

"No micros to drop off today, but I do have some questions about intake."

"I'm not sure how much I can help, kid."

"In that case, I'll keep it to one question: Did someone drop off a weather controller named Terrornado within the last hour?"

"Terrornado? Is that what that idiot at the school is calling himself?"

Of course Halpern was paying attention to goings-on at the academy. It's not only his job, but his daughter, Sarah, also goes to the school. I wonder if he's growing suspicious about his daughter finding herself at ground zero of all these metahuman incidents.

"That's him. So I take it you've got him?"

"Nope. Haven't had an intake in the last few days actually. Our ability to take in more than one or two metahumans at a time has been severely limited by, well, everything. I'd remember if anyone had come in today, especially a dummy with a bad name."

"Could he have been taken to another facility?"

Halpern takes out his phone and taps at the screen. "It's possible, but I doubt it. Even while operating under less than ideal conditions, Silver Island is still the safest place to bring criminal metahumans on the west coast. It wouldn't make sense to take a criminal from Skyville Academy anywhere else. The next closest facility is hundreds of miles away, and it doesn't do drop-offs, just containment."

"Can you tell me where the facility is? It's possible the meta I'm looking for was brought there instead."

"Sorry, classified location. And anyone who brings a metahuman directly to a classified location is turned away and told to leave in a less than pleasant manner. If a metahuman shows up on their doorstep without warning, security assumes it's an incoming attack and will defend itself accordingly."

Halpern taps on his phone again.

"Nope," he announces, "doesn't look like anyone anywhere has turned in any metahumans in the last few hours. It sounds like your new buddy, Terrornado, might be in the wind, no pun intended. Actually, I did intend that pun."

Only a few places on Earth can contain a metahuman with Terrornado's power. Whoever took him must have knocked him out first, but once Terrornado woke up, he wouldn't waste time before creating another weather anomaly with just a thought.

It looks like Silver Island is a dead end.

"Thanks for the help, Halpern."

"Don't mention it. Also, call next time. I'm going to catch hell for not telling you to leave the second you showed up."

"I will."

"Everything all right with you?"

"What do you mean?"

"Just because you're not dropping off bad guys anymore doesn't mean I don't follow the news. Unless I'm imagining things, I haven't seen you popping up much since Asana."

I glance down at my metabands and consider opening up to Halpern and telling him he's not crazy, that something is wrong. I want to tell him my metabands are failing, and I don't know how much longer they'll last. I want to tell him this might be the last time we speak and I appreciate everything he's done for me.

I open my mouth to speak, but then I hear Midnight's voice in my head.

Metaphorically.

He's warning me about trust. It's the reason he keeps his identity a secret and why he encourages me to do the same. According to him, staying alive is all about limiting who knows your weaknesses.

As Omni I'm strong, even with my metabands acting up.

But as Connor I'm vulnerable.

And I'm not the only one who's vulnerable either. The people I care about would be in danger if my identity was known. Revealing the truth about my damaged metabands would be similarly dangerous. If the wrong people learned I'm vulnerable, they'd come for me. Terrornado proved that. If I don't trust Halpern with my identity, why should I trust him with the knowledge my metabands are damaged?

"Yeah, everything's fine," I lie.

As I look up to take off into the sky, Halpern says, "Be careful out there, Omni."

"Of course."

"I'm not sure how you crossed paths with Terrornado, but he's a dangerous guy."

"If I wasn't crossing paths with dangerous guys, I wouldn't be doing my job right."

Halpern smirks. "I know, but this guy is different. He's a mercenary."

"He is?"

"That's one reason he's so hard to catch. There aren't any connections between him and his victims like there'd normally be. That's how we track down most meta criminals. Someone finds a pair of metabands, gains powers, and then decides to go after their old boss or ex-spouse and teach them a lesson. Or they go rob their bank or the closest mega mansion.

"But not this guy. He only shows up on our radar if someone else is paying him. I don't know all the details about what happened at Skyville Academy yet, but I can guarantee you one thing: Whoever Terrornado was after, he isn't the one who wants to see that person punished."

TWENTY-SEVEN

On my way back to the academy, I receive a text message from Michelle.

Come see me.

A message like that from Michelle usually means one thing. She doesn't have something to tell me; she wants to have a conversation. The difference might seem subtle, but now that I've known her for a while, the difference couldn't be starker.

While the message doesn't sound urgent, Michelle would not approve if she knew I was back on campus and ignoring her.

I'm flying low but fast above the woods on the outskirts of the academy. I'm close enough to scout for a place to land but far enough away that someone with regular vision won't likely spot me. The sun is setting, and most of the news trucks are gone. The remaining few are packing up for the day.

Nothing left to see here apparently.

The coast looks clear, so I set down along a hiking trail that cuts through the forest. I quickly deactivate my metabands and phase-shift them before jogging back toward campus. On the off chance I missed someone nearby, all they'd see is a student jogging through the woods.

I have no idea how I'd explain why I'm out here jogging in a pair of jeans, but I'm sure I could come up with something.

Maybe I ran here after Terrornado came and hid out for a couple of hours?

Sure, that'll work in a pinch.

Before I head back to school, there's someone else I want to talk to first.

KYLE OPENS his apartment door an instant before my knuckles can hit it. Alarmed, he glances around to see if I'm alone.

"Come inside," he says.

So far, this is easier than I thought.

He closes the door and breathes a sigh of relief. "Sorry, just a little paranoid. I'm guessing that goes away once you've been doing this for a while though, huh?"

"So it was you."

He laughs.

"Do you know anyone else with AI infused magtonium?"

"It's not funny. I almost got killed out there."

His brow furrows.

"I'm sorry. I didn't consider how terrifying that must have been for you, but everything worked out, and you're safe now. I'm just glad I was able to lend a hand."

"You didn't have anything to do with him showing up in the first place, did you?"

"I'm shocked you would even ask that. Of course not."

"Then what happened to Terrornado after you incapacitated him?"

"Relax, Connor. He's contained. You won't have to worry about him anymore."

"I checked with the metahuman containment facilities and none of them have any record of you bringing him in."

"You checked with *most* of the metahuman containment facilities. We have a handful in Kaldonia. This Terrornado person is being held at one of them. A metahuman has never escaped a Kaldonian metahuman containment center, which sadly, as you know, cannot be said about the containment facilities in the United States."

"You took him out of the country? You can't do that. He has rights."

"No, he doesn't. Not anymore. He forfeited his rights the moment he arrived on campus wielding a natural disaster. The faster everyone else understands that, the sooner we can fix all the real problems in this world."

"Is this what magtonium is really about? Giving yourself powers? I thought magtonium was supposed to save the world with clean energy?"

"Nothing I did today precludes it from serving that purpose. It's my father who is obsessed with extracting energy from the material, but its potential goes far beyond that."

"Like using it to fight metahumans?"

"Like using it to reshape the world. Why waste time extracting energy for things like electric cars when the material itself can be used as a means of transportation? Magtonium can change the way people move around the planet. A small amount of magtonium can envelop your body and take you from New York to Hong Kong a thousand times faster than flying on a jet. And who knows what else we might unlock in the future? What you saw today is just the beginning of its true capabilities."

"So, it wouldn't be used against metahumans?"

"It could be, but only when necessary."

"Who decides when it is necessary?"

"Kaldonia does."

"But Kaldonia already possesses the technology to keep metahumans outside its borders."

"That is a defensive strategy. It works now, but will it work forever? Who is to say an enemy won't one day circumvent our shield? Why are we only allowed a shield and not a sword of our own as well?"

"But do-"

"It is our right to exclude metahumans from our country, and with magtonium, we will have the best means yet to enforce that law. You may not like our rules, but when you are in Kaldonia, you will follow them. We are a sovereign nation, and we demand the right to possess offensive options to protect ourselves."

Kyle's voice has risen, and his face is growing red. I wait a beat to let him catch his breath, but I'm also a little nervous. He's speaking with a passion that borders on fervor.

"I just want you to be careful, that's all," I say.

"And why should I listen to you?"

"You don't have to, but I've been where you are, and my advice is to proceed with caution."

"How have you been where I am? You happened upon a pair of metabands, devices you don't know the first thing about. You became a superhero and an overnight celebrity through dumb luck. I've spent my life educating myself, learning through experimentation, trudging through trial and error, and I've finally cracked the mysteries of magtonium and unlocked its true power. I've spent countless nights harnessing artificial intelligence, and it was a hell of a lot harder than clicking two bracelets together."

Now my face is flushing.

He's smart, but even a genius doesn't know everything. He doesn't know everything about me, and he certainly doesn't know anything about the journey I've been through before finding these metabands. It wasn't dumb luck.

I swallow my pride, take a deep breath, and continue.

"You're right, but it seems like you think the hard part is over when it's really just beginning. This kind of power can be difficult to control despite having the best of intentions. You said it yourself: I've killed people. It's something I never wanted to do and could have never imagined. I learned the hard way it's something I'm capable of, and it's something I think about every single day. Hurting people is extremely easy to slip into, but nearly impossible to come back from."

"Well then, that's one area where we differ. I don't want to kill people either, but I'm willing if that's what it takes."

"What does that mean?"

"It means I've seen too much of the pain metahumans can cause. People like you and The Agency act like metahumans can be controlled. You take rules and laws meant for human beings and apply them to gods. You put the ones who misbehave in weak prisons, then act shocked when they escape. You try to reason with people who can kill dozens, hundreds, or thousands with a glance and pretend they can be reformed.

"They can't be, and the world is starting to realize that. It's time you stopped being so naive."

TWENTY-EIGHT

I leave Kyle's apartment angry and frightened. What if Kyle does something I can't stop?

Another text message pops up on my phone from Michelle telling me to come see her. I text back that I'm on my way.

I try to contact Midnight. My communicator is back online now, but it can't establish a connection with him. This worries me too. Midnight has answered my calls while literally in the middle of a fight. He either really has his hands full or isn't in the mood to talk.

The halls are deserted at the underground training facility. I check the time on my phone and see it's early evening. Usually the facility is filled with students finishing up their training, but it looks like no one's been here all day.

Michelle's office door is open a crack. She almost always has it closed. I knock and she tells me to come in.

Michelle is at her desk with her back to me, typing an email.

"Have a seat. I'll be with you in a second," she says.

I pull up one of the two armchairs across from her desk and sit.

When she finishes, she swivels her chair around to face me. She looks exhausted. I've never seen her like this before. Her appearance is always polished, a result of her borderline perfectionist personality.

"Tell me what happened today," she says.

"A lot, including some very interesting information I learned before heading over here."

"Start from the beginning, please."

"Well, the short version is that some idiot named Terrornado tried to kill me."

"I'm happy you're all right, Connor."

"Thanks, Michelle. Turns out he isn't just a run of the mill idiot with metabands, but a mercenary."

"Yes, I'm aware of that. Do you know who might have hired him?"

"If I had to guess, it's someone who isn't happy with how I handled Asana. It wasn't you, was it, Michelle?" I joke.

Michelle doesn't crack a smile. "This is serious, Connor."

"Sorry. I tend to use humor as a defense mechanism whenever I almost die, which is like all the time lately."

"That's why I wanted you to speak with you. Connor—"

"Look," I interrupt, "I knew what I was signing up for. If people aren't trying to kill me, that means I'm not doing my job right."

"There's a problem with that perspective because you're not only putting yourself at risk, and being a metahuman isn't your job. Your job is being a student. I'd hoped to teach you how to control and use your powers more effectively, but it's becoming increasingly obvious it's too much. Something has to give, and that something has been your studies and the safety of this campus."

"You're right. I'll try harder. No one died today, though, so ultimately—"

"We got lucky. Or rather, you got lucky. It's just a matter of time before your luck runs out, Connor. Running an underground training facility for metahumans who aren't even old enough to vote always carried that risk. When I accepted this position, I knew one day the worst might happen and I'd have to live with the consequences. I wasn't sure how I would do it, but I thought I'd gone into this with my eyes wide open.

"But today changed everything. Other students, regular students, were in danger. They aren't metahumans. They don't have metabands or superpowers. They don't know what they've signed up for by choosing Skyville Academy. They don't know their school serves as a cover for a metahuman training facility. I did my best to keep that a secret because I thought that was the best way to keep them safe. It was for a while, but it's not anymore. I'm shutting down the training program."

"You're what?"

"I'm shutting it down. The training facility, the response teams, all of it. There's too much risk, too much danger. I realized today that I couldn't have lived with myself if students had been killed. I couldn't have gone on with all the lies that keep this place operational. So I'm stopping it before I have to."

I'm quiet as I take on the weight of what Michelle is telling me. My mind is racing with counterarguments. What about the hypothetical number of innocent lives metahumans from the academy have saved thanks to their training? What about all the metahumans who might have turned down a darker path if it weren't for Michelle?

Despite the many arguments I could make, one look into Michelle's eyes tells me none of them will change her mind.

"I've already informed the other students. Most are taking a day to figure out what they want to do next. I suspect many will return home and re-enroll at their former high schools. If that isn't an option, such as in your case, or if they would prefer not to, they're still welcome here at Skyville. All scholarships and financial assistance will remain in place. This will be hard enough on many of them, and I don't want anyone to have to leave a school they've come to think of as a home because of my decision."

"That's generous of you."

Michelle waves this off. "It's the right thing to do. There is one important stipulation, though. Any student who wishes to remain at the academy must forfeit their metabands."

"But we're already prohibited from using them on school grounds."

"And that wasn't enough to keep this campus safe. Complete forfeiture of metabands is the only way to ensure the academy is never targeted again."

"But I didn't even use my metabands today."

"Exactly. Terrornado wasn't targeting Omni; he was targeting Connor Connolly. He knew you were the same person and came after you where you were most vulnerable. That's what made today's events so frightening."

"And I'm going to figure out how he found out who I am and who put him up to it."

"It doesn't matter. Even if you find out who sent Terrornado after you, there will be a next time. No one can live two separate lives forever. One will always bleed into the other. It's impossible for it not to."

"Midnight does it."

"No, he doesn't. Midnight doesn't lead two lives. He leads one. That mask is who he is, and that's how he ensures his identity is never a weakness."

"So that's the ultimatum? Give up my metabands for good or leave the school?"

"You don't have to give them up for good. What you do after graduation is up to you. You'd only be giving them up for a couple of years. In exchange, you can stay here and guarantee yourself admission to any college you want. It's a big decision, Connor, and I want you to make it on your own, but I also want to address the elephant in the room: your metabands are dying."

Hearing those words out loud stuns me.

"How do you know?"

"The same way you do. I don't have any secret knowledge. I haven't run any clandestine tests on them while you were asleep. Midnight hasn't shared anything we don't already know. I know they're dying because I'm watching it happen in real time."

"So you don't know anything about them. You're just guessing."

"Connor, please don't get defensive. Look, I've never worn metabands. I can't begin to understand what it feels like to possess such power, so I certainly can't understand what it would feel like to lose it."

"That makes two of us," I counter, unwilling to accept what Michelle is telling me.

Michelle pauses. She's frustrated, but she's trying not to let it get to her. "Why didn't you use your metabands today?"

"You told me I wasn't allowed to."

Michelle smiles.

"Connor Connolly, we both know there is no way in the world you would have listened to me while students were in danger. You might be in denial, but I know you don't think I'm stupid enough to believe that."

She's right, of course. Michelle knows I wouldn't have hesitated to use my metabands today if I could have. Instead of following this line of questioning to its logical conclusion, I change the subject.

"Do you know about the person who intervened today?"

"Kyle Toslov? Yes, we are aware of his involvement."

Michelle swivels in her chair and enters a few commands into her computer. The screen displays a large passport photo of Kyle alongside grainy surveillance video of today's attack.

"That was quick."

"He doesn't seem interested in protecting his identity."

"That tracks with what I've seen so far. I spoke to him before coming here, and he didn't seem concerned with keeping a low profile. I take it someone is planning an intervention?"

"It's complicated."

"What do you mean it's complicated? He's dangerous. He took Terrornado to Kaldonia, where he'll likely be sentenced without a trial and either executed on the spot or forced to a lifetime of hard labor. Kyle has no remorse for what he did and plans to keep doing it. He told me himself."

"But he isn't a metahuman."

"It doesn't matter. He has powers like one."

"But he isn't one. That's a big difference, legally speaking, and that isn't considering all the diplomatic issues."

"We barely have a diplomatic relationship with Kaldonia."

"I'm aware of that, Connor, but what would you have us do?"

"Tell Kyle he has to stop using his magtonium until we know more about it."

"And if he refuses? Would you want him arrested? He's the son of the dictator leading Kaldonia. His arrest would cause a major international incident and possibly lead to war."

"So, you're not doing anything?"

"We'll continue to monitor the situation and intervene where we can."

"Meanwhile, if I don't hang up my metabands, you'll throw me out of school?"

"They're different situations, Connor."

"They don't feel different."

My phone vibrates inside my pocket. I pull it out just as a large red window pops up on Michelle's computer monitor. I don't have to look at my phone to know the two alerts are connected.

"The FAA is reporting a damaged 747 is circling above Bay View City," Michelle says. "They're telling people to seek shelter."

I'm already walking out the door.

To hell with the consequences.

TWENTY-NINE

The campus is dark and empty. I concentrate on materializing my metabands, and when they appear around my wrists, relief floods through me.

"You there, Jim," I ask into my communicator.

After a few seconds of silence, there's a click and Jim replies, "Yeah, I'm here."

"Thank goodness. I'm pretty sure you're the only one I've got left."

"What does that mean?"

"I'll explain later. Are you tracking this 747?"

"Sure am. Latest radar data puts it ten thousand feet above Bay View City and about a mile north of downtown. Radio transmissions between the pilot and control tower aren't good, though. The plane is in too poor condition to return to its departure point, so they're redirecting it to a smaller airport outside the city."

"What are the odds of the plane making it?"

"There's a hole in the cabin and they've lost pressure. There's almost zero chance of it reaching either airport. I think they're trying to minimize collateral damage."

I look at my cracked metabands and my stomach sinks. I'm not sure if they're in any condition to power Omni, but I have to try. The fact they showed up is a decent sign. I close my eyes and send a quick prayer to anyone who's listening before I bring them together in front of my chest.

Light explodes as the metabands activate. Once my eyes have readjusted from the flash, I see it worked. Omni's suit is covering my body, and the metabands' energy is coursing through my body.

With a thought, I lift into the air.

I can still fly—for now, at least.

I orient myself toward the Bay View City skyline and push off.

I'm flying fast, but don't push it too hard. I'm afraid my metabands will fail if I put too much strain on them.

I soon spot the 747. It's a few miles out, but visible thanks to the fire and smoke streaming from one of its engines.

"I see it, Jim."

"Great. Now you just have to catch it in midair."

I increase my speed and approach. I was worried it'd be moving erratically, maybe spinning out of control, but it's traveling in a relatively straight line. Unfortunately, that straight line is pointed steeply at the ground.

"Any tips on how to grab this thing?" I ask Jim.

"Um, carefully?"

"Thank you, very helpful."

"You're acting like I've got experience catching 747s just because I knew where to find it."

"Can't you like, I don't know, pull up schematics?"

"That only works on TV."

Sigh.

"Right, I knew that."

"My non-sarcastic advice is to position yourself under the plane and push against it slowly. If you stop it all at once, you might push right through it. Remember, you're small, the plane's not."

"Got it."

I pull up next to the plane. I'm close enough to see in through the passenger windows. I'm surprised everyone looks calm inside the cabin. But what was I expecting to see? People running up and down the aisles with their hair on fire? They're falling from the sky and hanging on to whatever's closest to them for dear life.

When I get closer, the picture becomes clearer.

People are crying.

Some are hyperventilating.

There are terrified children and screaming babies.

I pull around to the nose of the plane and look into the cockpit. The pilots are trying to hold it together, but the expressions on their faces tell the truth. They think they're going to die.

The co-pilot glances up from the emergency procedure manual and catches sight of me. He excitedly hits the other pilot on the arm and points at me. Relief washes over both their faces.

I'm not sure how to communicate to them that they're not out of the woods yet. I'm sure the idea of a metahuman showing up to save them went through their minds, but they don't realize they've pulled the short straw with me.

As best I can, I motion for the pilot to pull back on the controls.

He looks back at me with a confused expression I interpret as, *What the hell do you think I've been trying to do?*

Never mind. The important thing is he knows I'm here. I don't want what happens next to startle him and cause him to fight against me. I speed up my descent and position myself under the plane, careful to match its speed so I don't rip through the hull like Jim warned.

I slowly approach the nose and place both hands on it. I can feel the violent vibrations reverberating throughout the plane's aluminum body and do my best to steady it.

Then comes the tricky part: slowing down the plane.

I take a deep breath and push against the plane's nose. It holds, and the vibrations seem to decrease. I hope that means I'm doing something right.

More confident, I further decelerate my fall and take on more of the plane's weight. Even though I'm exerting more energy, the plane isn't slowing down.

I glance at the city below. I'm not sure of our altitude, but I know one thing for sure: The city below is much bigger and closer than it was a minute ago.

Okay, it's not time to pull out all the stops yet, but I should start pulling out most of them.

Steadying myself against the nose, I lean forward and push harder, actively fighting against the plane, but it isn't working.

I place my shoulder against the nose, silently count to three, and push with all I've got.

The plane slows down!

Then my grip slips.

The tail whips around and nearly hits me.

Taking my hands off the nose and pushing with my shoulder may have given me more leverage, but it took away control. Without my hands to keep the plane centered, I'd pushed the plane off to one side and sent it into a dangerous tailspin.

I curse and grab at the tail as it spins past, but a piece comes off in my hands. I reposition myself and grab at it again more gently. It's hard to control my strength while in a panic. That's why Midnight always pushes me to train more. In times like these, I need to have full control over my powers.

My second attempt to grab the tail works, but now I'm spinning too. As carefully as possible, I counter the tail's momentum and pull it out of its spin. With the plane back to rocketing toward the Earth in a straight line, I fly back to the nose and try again.

I choose a different tactic and face away from the plane. I back up and rest the nose between my shoulder blades. Stretching both arms behind me, I grab onto either side of the plane's nose to steady it.

I slow my fall, and the full weight of the plane bears down on me. In this position, I have an excellent view of the city below, which I'm approaching at an alarming speed.

I must be ten seconds away from impact. If I don't do more, my chance to save the plane and its passengers will be over.

I take another deep breath, close my eyes, clench my teeth, and push harder than I ever have before.

The plane slows dramatically, and the city is no longer ten seconds away. Now it's maybe only twelve or thirteen seconds away.

Then the aluminum resting between my shoulders starts to buckle. I'm applying too much force for its structure to remain intact. The nose of a 747 is strong, but it isn't meant to support the plane's full weight.

More of the plane's nose crumples around me as I push farther and farther back into it. I'm risking another tailspin, so I dig my hands deep into the aluminum skin and grab the stronger steel skeleton underneath.

When I open my eyes, the city is too close. My powers are too weak.

We're going to crash.

THIRTY

I'm screaming with effort when my grip is flung off from the plane. Pieces of the aluminum hull are wrapped tightly in my fists, and a skyscraper is approaching fast.

How did I lose my grip? I apply what I think of as airbrakes and narrowly avoid colliding with the building. Once I have my momentum back under control, I turn and push back toward the falling plane.

Except the plane isn't falling anymore. It's suspended in midair.

That must be why it felt like I'd been flung from it. It stopped falling, but I didn't stop pushing.

I approach quickly to see what was going on, nervous to see if the plane is still in danger, but then I see what stopped the plane in its tracks.

Kyle.

He's wearing the black magtonium like a suit of armor and calmly holding the plane over his head by its midsection. The magtonium pulls away from his face, and he says with a wink, "Looked like you needed a hand."

He descends from the sky with the plane held over his

head. He makes it look easy. He nods, motioning for me to follow him to the ground.

It takes me a few seconds to follow. I'm struggling to catch my breath and mentally check in with my metabands. My wrists feel like they're on fire. I have to land before these things deactivate on their own.

Kyle is easing the plane down onto a highway beneath me. He's strong enough to reposition himself and turn the plane with ease. Cars and trucks screech to a stop. Some make U-turns across multiple lanes of traffic to get away from the surreal scene. I see the lights and hear the sirens of approaching emergency vehicles.

Kyle shouts up at me as I approach.

"I know this isn't the most ideal place to leave a 747, but I don't think it's wise to risk flying it anywhere else. The nose is in horrible shape, and I'm afraid its structure will collapse under any more strain. Pro tip for next time, Connor. Grab underneath. The belly is built to endure the most strain."

"Omni."

"What?"

"Don't call me that out here."

Kyle shrugs. "I just saved your ass. I think that entitles me to call you whatever I want tonight."

With both feet on solid ground again, I swipe at my metaband and the indicator tells me what I already know: They're drained and on the verge of failing.

I desperately want to power them down to preserve what little energy is left, but with Kyle announcing my first name to anyone within earshot, I decide it's best to keep my face covered.

That doesn't mean I'm letting this go without an argument.

Kyle pulls the door off the plane with ease and tosses it aside. Inside, the crew and terrified passengers are waiting. Upon seeing Kyle, they break into applause. He waves as the emergency exit slide is deployed. As he returns to the ground, a yellow streak tears across the sky.

Great. Now I'll have to rely on Kyle to save my butt again if this person is looking for a fight.

The streak crashes in front of us, kicking up dust and asphalt. Through the cloud of debris, a figure emerges and runs toward us.

"Whoa, easy," I say as I put my hands up, ready to defend myself.

"No, no, no! I'm sorry. I'm so sorry. I'm not here to hurt you, I swear," the man says.

He's clad from head to toe in yellow. If his dropping out of the sky wasn't a big enough clue, then the bands around his wrists confirm he's a metahuman.

"Who are you?" I ask.

"Joe. My name is Joe Stapleton. I'm just a regular guy. I found these metabands tonight and gave them a try, but I have no idea what I'm doing. I wanted to fly, but it was way too fast. I started panicking, and that just made it worse."

"Where are you going with this, Joe?" I ask.

I want to get out of here ASAP. I don't trust my metabands not to deactivate and expose my identity to a plane full of witnesses. I'd be surprised if anyone recognized Connor Connolly, but they'd certainly realize I'm a teenager. That fact alone would spread like wildfire and provide anyone interested in my true identity with more clues.

I don't have time to give a new metahuman a tutorial on flying tonight.

"I saw the plane in the sky and stayed away, but these

stupid metabands must have thought I was looking at it because I wanted to fly to it."

Oh no.

"And?"

"And I flew into it," Joe stammers, his voice cracking. "I crashed into the plane. I'm so, so sorry. You must understand I never meant for this to happen. I'm so happy you saved them. If you hadn't been there to fix my screw-up, I don't know what I would have—"

Joe Stapleton goes quiet. His mouth hangs open as he struggles to speak. I look down at his chest and stagger back in disbelief.

Protruding from his chest is a black and red blade. It's moving as though it were alive. Behind Joe stands Kyle, his arm transformed into a weapon.

"What are you doing!" I scream.

I run to help Joe. In the back of my mind, I know it's too late, but my instinct is to help, no matter how futile it might be. Before I can reach him, Kyle casually flicks his wrist and tosses Joe fifty yards down the highway. I watch in horror as his body hits the pavement and bounces lifelessly before skidding to a stop.

"I'm doing what needs to be done," Kyle says. He looks down at the arm he transformed into a blade and shakes it. The blood is hurled onto the pavement with a sickening splat. "That man killed people."

"No, he didn't! It was an accident. You didn't even listen to him."

"I didn't need to. And he did kill people. I saw them on my way here. Three passengers in total. They were ripped from their seats and sucked out of the hole your friend punched into the plane after he decided to take his new metabands out for a joyride."

The news is crushing. Three innocent people were dead, people I had no chance of saving. They spent the last few seconds of their lives in confused terror as they hurtled toward the Earth. It's no way to go.

"That doesn't mean Joe deserved to die."

"Tell me, then, what did he deserve?"

"He deserved better. A trial. Justice. Not an execution in the streets."

"What he deserved is irrelevant. This is about sending a message. Metabands aren't toys, and I'm tired of people treating them as such. Everyone, the government, the media, they act as though those pieces of metal are the answers to all our prayers. What have they gotten us? Thousands killed. Even more injured or maimed. And for what? So a handful of self-proclaimed do-gooders can play superhero while the rest of us deal with the aftermath?"

The small group of passengers gathered around us applaud. For a moment, I think the applause is a thank-you for saving their lives, but it's not.

A man points down the street at Joe Stapleton's body and gives Kyle a thumbs-up.

They're not thanking Kyle for saving them; they're thanking him for killing the metahuman who caused the crash.

Kyle grins and waves.

"It's not that simple," I say.

"You're right, it's not. But it can be. An eye for an eye. That's true justice."

"What gives you the right to decide? Because you're rich? Because you're the son of a dictator? You think that makes you better than everyone else? You think that gives you the right to decide who dies!" I scream.

There's a beep in my ear. Jim is calling in, but I tap on

the communicator and cancel the connection. I notice the indicator on my metabands is flashing red.

Everything around me is falling apart, yet Kyle is still smirking.

"There it is. That's what I was waiting for. I'm glad I didn't have to hire another mercenary to get you to stop biting your tongue and say what you really think."

"You sent Terrornado after me? What is wrong with you?"

"Going after you was his idea. I merely hired him so I'd have an easy target to make my first public example."

"You're sick. There's something wrong with you, Kyle. I don't know if it's the magtonium causing it or what, but you need to stop all of this right now."

"See, killing isn't always such a bad thing. In the face of death, many are motivated to speak their minds for the first time. I'm glad all our cards are on the table now." Magtonium from Kyle's shoulders moves up his face and envelops his head, leaving only his mouth and jawline exposed. "I'm done here. I suggest you make yourself scarce too." He points at my wrist. "That blinking light can't be a good sign."

He rockets into the night sky, and in a matter of seconds, he's out of sight.

Still in a state of shock, I tell myself I need to get out of here before my metabands fail. Incidents like this tend to attract other metahumans, and in this shape, I wouldn't last longer than five seconds in a fight.

I squint at the nearest street sign. I know exactly where I am and how to get out of here.

THIRTY-ONE

I'm a few blocks from Derrick's apartment, but the indicators on my metabands are flashing bright red. I'm not sure I'll make it. I've never run them down this low before, and I'm freaking out about what will happen if they fail while active. I assume the maroon-colored Omni uniform will recede into the bands and my powers will stop working, but I might be missing other possibilities.

I've always been afraid of letting them fail for a few reasons. For starters, they need downtime to recharge. If they're ever drained completely, they might not have enough energy to recharge themselves.

I think of this as the "car battery" model of charging. As long as they have a charge left, they can always fully recharge themselves. If you let a car battery die, say by accidentally leaving your lights on, the car can't start to recharge its battery.

I know this because Derrick's done it. Twice. In the same week.

You can give the battery a jump-start, but if there's a

way to jump-start a pair of dead metabands, no one's figured it out yet.

There are stories of metas draining their metabands. Few want to admit such a dumb mistake, so information is sketchy at best. Some claim to have powered them on again after a long period of rest. The difference between those metabands and mine, though, is the damage mine have sustained. Mine haven't been the same since my fight with the Alphas, and no one, not even Midnight, can explain why.

Maybe I'm worrying about the wrong thing. Maybe if mine run out of juice, they won't turn off at all, and instead of turning back into "Connor," I'll be stuck as Omni forever, unable to remove the dead metabands from my wrists.

Maybe they'll explode.

Maybe they'll create a black hole and suck me into it.

It all sounds crazy, but so do bracelets that let you fly.

The growing mob is gawking at the crashed 747. In fairness, it's not every day that a 747 crash lands in the middle of a downtown intersection, but it's creating a headache for me since I can't find a safe place to power down.

Some give me strange glances as I walk past. You don't often see a metahuman hobbling down the street. No flight, no super speed, just a metahuman limping around. The stares don't last long, though. Everyone in Bay View City knows who Omni is, and no one expects to see him walking down the street. Most of them assume I'm some weirdo dressed up in very accurate cosplay.

I'm not about to do anything to convince them otherwise.

I keep an eye out for Derrick, half-expecting to find him running down the street toward the crash site, but as I get closer to his apartment building, the crowd thins significantly. Derrick has monitored police and emergency services radio frequencies to chase down stories, but I guess he isn't doing it tonight.

On his block, the street is essentially empty. I find a narrow alley between a pizzeria and a bookstore, two places that are less likely to have exterior security cameras than say a bank. A quick check along the alley's walls confirms the lack of cameras, and I bring my metabands together to power them down.

There's a crackle of electricity and a blinding flash. I'm knocked back several feet into a pile of garbage bags.

Well, that's new.

I rub my eyes as I pull myself onto my feet. My metabands are in worse shape than ever. They're charred black. There's no smoke or smell emanating from them, but it's obvious that tonight has further damaged them.

Regardless of what they look like, I need to hide them.

I try to phase-shift them, but nothing happens.

I close my eyes and try again.

It's no use.

My heart skips a beat at the thought this might be it. They might finally be toast.

Don't panic. Try to think rationally about this.

I consider banging them together to see if they still work, but if they're not dead, they're certainly on their last legs. Powering them up now might push them over the edge.

I better not risk it.

I pull the metabands off my wrists and stuff them into my hoodie pockets. It's not as convenient as phasing them into a different dimension, but it'll have to do.

I poke my head out of the alley to check for any curious passersby who might have heard the huge boom from my metabands, but the street is still empty. I hurry toward Derrick's building a few buildings down.

As I enter through the large glass doors, the concierge seated at the front desk remarks, "Hey, Mr. Connolly! Long time, no see."

"Yeah, been busy at school, unfortunately," I reply, hoping to keep the small talk to a minimum.

I'm not completely lying. I have been away at school, but he hasn't seen me in a while because it's easier to come and go through the roof. I feel a tinge of sadness when I realize I might be using the front door from now on.

"Of course. You're at that fancy-pants academy. We'll all be calling you boss one day, I'm sure," the concierge jokes.

I'm tempted to tell him that's unlikely since I'll probably be expelled. Instead, I simply offer a friendly smile as I head to the elevator and insert the key for Derrick's penthouse apartment.

The elevator whisks me up to the forty-seventh floor.

The door opens, and I walk right into Derrick as he steps in.

I bounce off his chest and say, "Good timing."

"Connor! Thank goodness you're all right," he says.

Derrick steps back into the apartment. I follow, and the elevator door closes behind me.

He looks so relieved I'm surprised he doesn't throw his arms around me.

"I'm all right, relatively speaking."

"I just heard. That's where I was going."

Derrick and I walk into his living area. He notices I'm limping and offers his arm. I brush it away, insisting I'm fine.

The massive television screen mounted to the living

room wall is displaying live footage from the crash scene alongside cell phone videos taken by eyewitnesses. There's a warning on the lower third of the screen about graphic content.

"I assume you know the basics," I say, gesturing at the TV.

"A metahuman caused a plane crash, but you and this new guy stopped it."

"That new guy is Kyle Toslov."

"What? He's a metahuman? When did that happen?"

"He's not a metahuman. That stuff covering his body is magtonium infused with artificial intelligence. Magtonium isn't some inert material; it's nanotechnology. That suit is essentially a bunch of supercharged nanobots working together to give him the same abilities as a metahuman. He developed the AI himself."

Derrick looks dumbfounded as he plops onto the couch, scratching the top of his head. "I'm not sure I understand."

"That makes two of us."

"And the person he killed?"

"Just some guy who found metabands and didn't know how to use them. He collided into the plane and three passengers were sucked out. They'd hit the ground before I even heard about the accident."

"If it was an accident, why did Kyle kill him?"

"To send a message. He thinks there needs to be harsher consequences for metahumans who causes these types of incidents."

As Derrick takes it all in, I glance at the television. The news channel has switched from live coverage of the scene to an in-studio anchor seated alongside a panel of guests. Though they're discussing the crash, a few members of the panel look happy. I pick up the remote and unmute the television.

"... what a lot of people have been saying all along. Metahumans are dangerous and have been acting with impunity for way too long," a panelist says.

"Don't we already have the tools within our legal system to deal with metahumans?" the anchor asks.

"Our legal system is meant for human beings. We could never have imagined we'd have to one day deal with metahumans who can cause the level of damage previously reserved for military warfare. Look at the incident on Silver Island. We've tried to treat these metahumans like human beings and it blows up in our faces over and over again. Once you bond with a pair of metabands, you're no longer human in my book. You're a meta. The rules change, and we, as a society, need to catch up. That's what Judgment has shown us tonight."

"Judgment?" the anchor asks.

"Sorry," the panelist says through a smile, "that's what people online are calling the hero who saved those passengers today."

"Would it be inaccurate to credit him alone in that feat? Many witnesses reported the metahuman known as Omni also aided in the rescue."

"You mean the same Omni who not only caused the Silver Island breakout, but also the nuclear contamination at Asana just days ago?"

"Allegedly."

"You can say allegedly all you want, but we all know his ineptitude led to both events. That plane was about to crash into downtown Bay View City before Judgment showed up. We all saw it. And what about Omni's failure to act when the perpetrator of the crash returned to the scene of the crime? He likely would have let him go, just like he let those prisoners go from Silver Island. If you ask me, Omni's lucky Judgment didn't take those matters into his own hands right then and there."

The television turns off. Derrick is holding the remote control.

"That's enough," he says.

THIRTY-TWO

"What are we going to do?" I ask, following Derrick into the kitchen. He pours me a large glass of water, and I greedily accept it. I didn't realize how dehydrated I am. Catching a plane with broken metabands took a lot more out of me than I thought.

Derrick grabs himself a bottle of beer from the refrigerator. I pull out my phone and shoot Jim a message, letting him know I'm okay and will talk to him tomorrow.

"What do you mean?" Derrick asks.

"What are we going to do about Kyle, or Judgment, or whatever he calls himself?"

"I'm not sure. Have you been able to get in touch with Midnight?"

"No."

"Me neither. I thought he was ignoring my calls, but I don't think he'd ignore you too, not with everything that's going on."

"Do you think he's okay?"

"No way to know for sure. None of my sources have reported any sightings, but he's gone dark before. I wouldn't worry too much until we know more. It's more important we focus on the immediate threat here. Speaking of which, I'm guessing Judgment knows your identity?"

"Yeah, he figured it out a while ago."

"Do you think he'll come after you?"

"He could've killed me tonight, but he didn't."

"That's true. What happened out there?"

"I'll show you."

I grab my sweatshirt off the back of Derrick's couch and pull out my metabands from the pockets.

"Holy crap. This happened tonight?"

"Not all of it. They started acting up after the fight with the Alphas, but it got worse after Asana. Obviously, it's not good."

"Can I hold them? Are they safe to touch?"

"Um, I guess so."

I hand the metabands over to Derrick, and he grabs them hesitantly, like he's expecting a static shock.

"I've never seen anything like this," Derrick says.

"That makes two of us. They haven't been the same since Silver Island. The hairline cracks have been getting worse, and they almost failed on me tonight. I've never let their energy level get so low before. Most of the damage happened after I powered them down."

"Do they still work?"

"I'm too afraid to power them up. I'll have to sooner or later, though. If they're busted, I'd rather find out now than when I need them. I wish I could talk to Midnight. If anyone's seen metabands acting like this, it'd be him."

"I'll keep trying to reach him. In the meantime, I think you should stay out of sight."

"This isn't a great time to be doing that."

"There's never a good time, but that's irrelevant. You

can't rely on these things to work, so you need to avoid situations where you might need them. Michelle told me about the talk she had with you today."

"Way to change the subject."

"I'm not trying to change the subject. If you'd let me finish, I was going to point out that since you won't be at the academy for the foreseeable future, your chances of running into Judgment will be greatly reduced, but only *if* you lie low and take it easy. You're in no shape for a confrontation anyway."

"You don't know that."

Derrick holds up the charred metabands. "Your metabands look like a burnt marshmallow."

"They're indestructible. They might need some downtime to recharge and repair themselves, but they'll come back around."

"It's not just Judgment you have to worry about. Others aren't too happy with you over what happened at Asana. Thanks to Kyle, you're probably on the Kaldonian government's naughty list too."

"What are they going to do? They're the size of Rhode Island."

"Rhode Island is a lot bigger than you are, Connor. I wouldn't put a lone kid with a pair of busted metabands up against an entire nation's army, no matter how small they are."

"So, I'm just a kid now?"

"You know what I mean. I just want what's best for you. You've got to be exhausted after these past few days. You can stay here and rest up. I'm getting coffee with Michelle tomorrow. I'll talk to her about the academy. I'm sure once all this blows over, she'll let you back in."

"It won't just blow over. You don't know Kyle. He's

committed, and he's determined. He gave himself these powers through sheer force of will. You should see the lab in his apartment. This wasn't some freak accident. He set a goal and achieved it. Now he has another plan: wiping out any metahuman he thinks deserves it. He won't stop until he does it."

"You can't know that for sure. This was his first public appearance. He was probably so hopped up on adrenaline he didn't know what he was doing. We've seen it happen with new metahumans before. Most of them come around and settle down after the rush wears off."

"But he's not a metahuman. That's what I'm trying to explain to you. Why are you defending him? He's a murderer."

"I'm not defending him, Connor. I'm trying to stop you from doing something stupid and getting yourself hurt."

Derrick's cell phone lights up on the kitchen counter. He grabs it, reads the screen, and sighs. "The guy Judgment killed tonight, Joe Stapleton? Turns out he was under investigation for massive financial crimes: tax evasion, fraud, a whole bunch of stuff. Looks like he wasn't such a nice guy after all."

"That doesn't mean he deserved to die."

"I didn't say he did, but this just turned into an even bigger story. The reaction online to his death is largely positive. Judgment is trending on every social media platform. I'll have to head into the office."

Derrick reluctantly pours his untouched beer down the drain and tosses the bottle into the recycling bin.

"Will you be okay here by yourself for a while?"

"Yeah, I'll be fine."

"Do me a favor and please don't do anything stupid. I won't give you a big speech and threaten you to stay put.

You're a big boy, and I know you won't listen to me either way, but please, I'm asking you as your brother, just rest tonight. Stay here. The world will be here tomorrow when you wake up."

I give him a noncommittal nod and plop down on the couch as he grabs his coat from the hall closet.

"Don't watch too much news either. It's bad for your brain."

"Great advice from a reporter."

"Who would know better than me? I'll text you when I'm on my way back."

Derrick closes the door behind him, and I'm alone. I flip through the channels, looking for something to distract me, but all I can think about is the look on Joe Stapleton's face when Kyle stabbed him through his back. It'll haunt me for a while. And Judgment trending online isn't easing my mind either.

Kyle was born into unbelievable wealth and luxury in a country full of impoverished people.

But that isn't what bothered Kyle. He hated that others had something he wanted: the power of being a metahuman.

Now that he has powers of his own, it still isn't enough. He needs to dictate to the world who is and isn't worthy of possessing these abilities. If he finds someone unworthy, he needs to be the one who punishes them.

With others behind him and egging him on, I worry about what that will do to his head. He's already demonstrated many egotistical tendencies. I can't imagine what having millions of strangers telling him he's right will lead to.

His online supporters will grow bored in time. They

always do. What is Kyle willing to do to keep their attention?

After flipping through more TV channels than I knew existed, I give up and turn off the TV. Despite the long and eventful day, I can't stop fidgeting. I'm so tired I could fall asleep on my feet, but I can't sit still, and my mind won't shut off. I'm overtired, and my body is confused about whether it should rest or stay on high alert.

I pace back and forth in Derrick's living room, unable to stop going over today's events. On the verge of driving myself crazy, I walk over to the floor-to-ceiling windows to distract myself. The view is insane. It always reminds me of flying. The city feels so quiet and peaceful from high up.

I look for the plane's emergency landing site before realizing this window is facing the wrong way. Good. I can't take my mind off of things if I'm staring right at the ground zero of my current problems.

I take a deep breath and close my eyes. My heart rate is finally slowing and some of the tension is leaving my shoulders. Maybe all the adrenaline in my system was magnifying my angst. Maybe I'll be able to sleep tonight after all. I open my eyes.

Then I see it.

A streak is moving through the sky. It passes directly over Derrick's building, soaring toward the city limits. It would be too fast to identify if it weren't for one detail: the blur trailing behind it is purple.

Iris.

It has to be her. It's been weeks since anyone has heard from her, but some other random purple metahuman flying right over Derrick's apartment would be too much of a coincidence.

Before I can second-guess it, I run to the kitchen and grab my metabands off the counter.

Derrick has a strict, but understandable, rule about my metabands, which boils down to no metabands inside the house. It's modeled after the rule our parents set about not playing ball inside the house. The rule went into effect after Derrick threw a touchdown clean through our living room window.

Well, Derrick isn't here to enforce his rules, and I have no time to spare if I want to catch up with her.

Plus, I need to figure out if these metabands still work.

I hastily slip them around my wrists and squeal with joy when I feel them tighten around my wrists.

Thanks, guys. I promise we'll take it nice and easy tonight.

I bring the metabands together. After a few sparks and a slight delay, they activate. The Omni suit spreads over my body, and I'm ready to go. Even without checking the indicator, I can feel I'm nowhere near one hundred percent charged, but otherwise, it feels good.

I unlatch the nearest window and leap into the night, following the purple blur wherever she's taking me.

THIRTY-THREE

We're far outside the city, and I have the stupid idea this would be a better place for my metabands to fail while I'm in the air. As if landing in a field instead of on top of a building would make a difference while a few thousand feet above the ground.

I still don't know if the person I'm chasing is Iris. I've kept my distance to find out where she's going, but my gut tells me it's her. I just hope she's not flying to the North Pole or something, because there definitely isn't a lot of gas left in my tank.

The night is quiet, and the cold air is bothering me more than usual. I chalk it up to my reduced powers. The sky's calm, and there isn't any wind to fight against. Below, the houses are growing farther and farther apart as the chase continues.

I get lost in watching the fir trees passing under me. When I look up again, the purple streak is lower in the sky and slowing down.

Iris must be coming in for a landing. Thank goodness, because I'm rolling the dice flying this high.

A house comes into view. *House* is a misleading way of describing it. Even the word *mansion* sells this thing short. It looks like a structure you'd store other mansions inside. That's how big it is. If it weren't so far out in the country, I would assume it was an apartment building or mall.

As I get closer to the house, I lose sight of the purple streak, but there's nowhere else she could have gone. The surrounding area is dense forest, except for a single-lane road leading to the house.

A handful of lights are on inside the building. I imagine keeping the lights on in this place costs more than most peoples' mortgages, even though I don't really understand what a mortgage is. I just know it's something Derrick is always complaining about, like someone forced him to buy a multi-million dollar penthouse apartment.

Okay, it was somewhat my idea, but that's why you shouldn't let a sixteen-year-old influence your home-buying decisions.

I consider where to land and decide to point myself at the front door. Sometimes, a direct approach is best.

The landing is rougher than usual; I basically fall out of the sky. Luckily, I'm only about ten feet off the ground, but it still isn't my most graceful moment.

Conscious of how delicate my metabands are, I power them down, even though I'm worried they might not power back up. They need to recharge and repair themselves if they can, and keeping them active will prevent that from happening.

Plus, knocking on the door looking like a regular person will be less intimidating than showing up as a metahuman in a skintight, bright red, full body jumpsuit.

The front door is so massive it wouldn't fit in Derrick's

apartment. It has a big black iron doorknocker with a scary lion face. I have to be honest; it looks pretty cool. I grab the knocker and swing it into the door, producing a satisfyingly loud *knock-knock-knock*.

Well, if nothing else, I get to cross that off my bucket list.

I press my ear against the door, but I don't hear any movement inside. The door's probably too thick to hear anything through anyway.

After coming all the way out here, I won't let a door thwart me. I step back and scan the front of the house. None of the rooms on this side have any lights on. Frustrated, but not ready to give up, I walk around to the other side to see what I can find.

The moon is out, which is great. Otherwise, it'd be pretty dark this far in the countryside. As I make my way along the side of the building, I notice details that weren't apparent from the sky.

Mainly, this place is kind of a mess.

There are huge patches of exposed brick where the white paint is chipped. Dead strands of brown grass come up to my knees. Huge vines, so thick they obscure some of the windows, crawl up the side of the building. I assumed someone is living here from the few lights on in the house, but the lack of maintenance is giving me doubt.

How long can a lightbulb stay lit?

"What are you doing here?" a voice calmly asks.

I scream—loudly—and spin around. She's standing there with her arms crossed, looking pissed off.

It's Iris after all.

"What am I doing here? What are you doing here?" I ask.

"You followed me, so I get to ask the questions."

"Um, okay, in that case, I'm here because I followed you. My turn."

Iris keeps her arms crossed. She never thinks I'm funny.

"Why did you follow me?" she asks.

"Because no one's seen or heard from you in a while."

"So?"

"So, when you flew over Derrick's apartment, I figured you were telling me to follow you."

"That sounds like the justification of a stalker."

"I'm not a stalker. And I usually suck at following people."

"Well, I'm fine. End of story. I assume you can find your own way back."

She turns and heads toward the front of the house.

"Um ..." I jog to catch up with her. "I think I need a breather before I can power up and get out of here."

"A breather? Are you serious?"

"My metabands have been on the fritz lately."

I roll up the sleeves of my sweatshirt. She stops in her tracks, grabs the metaband on my right wrist, and yanks it up to her face for a closer examination.

She runs her fingers over the surface of the band. "Well, that's something you don't see every day."

"So, you live here alone?" I ask while she twists my wrist back and forth.

Iris doesn't answer. She lets go of the metaband and my arm falls back to my side. "How did this happen?"

"Wear and tear?"

"They're supposed to be indestructible."

"They're supposed to be, but something happened to mine at Silver Island. Since then, they've been getting worse. Same with my abilities. I was surprised they powered on at all."

"Interesting." She's silent for a long time, thinking. "You can stay here until they charge back up, *if* you promise to keep your weird questions to a minimum."

"I promise I'll try."

THIRTY-FOUR

"So, seriously though, whose place is this?"

We've been inside Iris's mansion for approximately three seconds.

Iris sighs. "I thought I warned you about asking questions."

"You said no *weird* questions. Asking how you came to live in a mansion the size of a small town is a normal question about a weird thing."

The mansion is as impressive on the inside as it is on the outside. The huge circular foyer has a massive chandelier in bad need of a dusting. Multiple hallways branch off the central one to other parts of the house.

"It belonged to someone who made a lot of money selling metabands to some very bad people. One of those people got pissed off after he bought a pair of metabands that didn't give him the abilities he wanted. Long story short, the metaband dealer isn't around to use his mansion anymore, and it seemed silly to let it go to waste."

"Yeah, but someone has to own it, right? Next of kin or something?"

"We've been here for months and haven't heard so much as a peep. As I'm sure you've noticed, we're far from civilization up here. Not many neighbors. The house was built and paid for by shell corporations inside of shell corporations. Other than the owner, few people know it's up here, and he barely used it."

"You said *we've* been here?"

"Who is this guy, Iris?" a gruff voice asks.

I nearly jump out of my skin.

Standing next to me is a guy roughly my age, maybe a little older. He's wearing jeans and a t-shirt, and his long black hair comes down to his shoulders. His shoulders are where he stops looking like a normal human being.

Bulging out of his sleeves are the most gigantically muscular arms I've ever seen. They look out of place on his otherwise skinny frame, like they've been grafted onto his body.

I try not to stare, but it's impossible. Unless there's some new fitness craze I'm not aware of, there's no way those arms are natural.

"John, this is Connor, an old friend. Connor, this is John Armstrong," Iris says.

John offers me his massive paw of a hand to shake. My brain screams at me not to take it since he looks like he could crush me without breaking a sweat, but I don't want to be rude.

"Nice to meet you. John Armstrong, huh? I bet they call you Strongarm, don't they?"

His grip around my hand tightens.

"Sorry, I'm sure you hear that all the time. I tend to make obvious jokes."

"They don't call him anything," Iris says. "John's not a metahuman."

I hadn't noticed until Iris said it, but John isn't wearing metabands.

"Wait, you're telling me you're this jacked, like, normally?" I ask.

"Not exactly," he replies. "It was nice meeting you, Connor." John Armstrong releases my hand and exits down a long dark hallway.

"Sorry about that," I say to Iris.

"My rule about asking weird questions extends to everyone in this house."

"Got it. In fairness, I didn't think it was *that* weird. How the hell is he so ripped if he's not a metahuman?"

"That's something we're all trying to figure out, and not just about John either."

"What do you mean?"

"Obviously, I'm not the only one living here. I didn't even find this place. In a way, they kinda found me."

"Who are they?"

"It changes from day to day. It's not a formal group or anything. Just a bunch of people in the same situation, trying to find answers."

"And that situation is...?"

Iris looks around to see if anyone's within earshot. "I'm not supposed to say. There aren't many rules, but keeping details about this place secret is one of them."

"Well, you already let me in. I assume that breaks the rule about secrecy."

"It's a place for people like me."

"You mean metahumans?"

"I'm not a metahuman. Or I am, I guess, but not the same way you are. My abilities don't come from a pair of metabands. I just have them."

"Wait, you're telling me there are others like you?"

"Yeah, a few. I'm among the lucky ones, if you could say that. My powers are all pretty useful, or at the very least they're not much of a burden. They're similar to yours. Flight, invulnerability, speed. They're abilities no one knows I have unless I show them. Most people who come in and out of here don't have that luxury."

"People like John?"

"He's one of them. When people dream about having super strength, they don't imagine having arms so large they can't walk down the street without people staring or making stupid jokes."

"Now I feel really bad. Will you tell him I'm sorry if I don't see him again?"

"Sure, he'll appreciate that. He knows people can't help how they react, but that doesn't make it any easier to constantly hear about it. Maybe one day, things will change and he'll embrace his arms and use his strength to help people, but right now, he just wants to live a normal life.

"That's the case for most people here. Many of them have undergone unexpected changes that seem to be permanent. Many have families that don't understand. That's how they wound up here."

"How am I just hearing about this now?"

"It's not something they want made public. Some of us are out there helping people, masquerading as metahumans, but most want to be left alone."

"What are they afraid of? Most people with metabands don't hide in the shadows. What's the big difference?"

Iris squints at me. "They're not hiding; they're living their lives. Not everyone wants to run around the city, fighting crime in their underwear."

"It's not underwear. If anything, it's more like pajamas."

That actually gets a small smirk out of Iris.

"Metabands aren't a physical part of their owners. Put them on your wrists, turn them on, get powers. When you're done, just turn them off. Scientists have been puzzling out how they work since before we were born, and so far, they've gotten almost nowhere. Because they're indestructible, taking them apart to figure out how they tick isn't an option.

"Human beings, however, are not indestructible. They can experiment on someone like John all they want; all they need is a scalpel to get started."

"Has that happened?"

"There are rumors of people disappearing. People are afraid of the unknown. Society is still afraid of metaband-powered metahumans. If they knew about humans *born* with abilities? It wouldn't be pretty."

"You're probably right. So, any idea where these abilities came from?"

"Most of them—*us*—have at least one parent who possessed metabands."

"Oh, wow, that makes sense. It's long been theorized that metabands alter their owner's DNA, so of course those alterations could be passed onto their offspring."

"Huh, and here I heard you weren't doing so hot at school."

"Hey, I pay attention sometimes. Wait, who told you how I've been doing in school?"

"Midnight."

"He knows about all this?"

"Duh. He found the house and figured out that our abilities are hereditary."

"You couldn't have figured that out on your own?"

"We're lucky to know at least one of our parents. Being a metahuman isn't exactly conducive to raising kids.

Some of them were orphaned at a young age. Others are the result of one-night stands. The whole secret identity thing makes tracking down metahuman parents much harder."

"Why didn't Midnight tell me about this?"

"Why hasn't he told you half the things you later found out on your own? He's not the best at sharing information he thinks isn't need to know."

"Speaking of which, when is the last time you talked to him?"

"It's been a few weeks."

"Damn, I was hoping it'd be more recent. I've had trouble reaching him over the past few days."

"That's not unusual."

"No, but I could really use his help right now."

"You don't have to tell me, I saw the shape your metabands are in."

"Hold on, if the first wave of metahumans passed down abilities, why do I need metabands? My parents were both metahumans."

"That's what I mean when I said there's a lot we don't understand. Abilities aren't always passed down to the offspring. Even when they are, the abilities aren't always the same. Maybe you found your pair of metabands before your latent abilities could present themselves and change something in you. Most abilities don't manifest until during or after puberty."

"Are you implying I haven't gone through puberty yet?"

"I'm not implying anything. I'm telling you what I know. It's also possible the metabands have to be active at the time of conception."

"All right, I think that's as much as I want to think about that."

"Well, ask a weird question, get a weird answer. Are you hungry?"

"Now that you mention it, I'm starving."

"I'll show you to the kitchen."

"You're gonna make me something?"

"This isn't your fancy private school. You can make a sandwich yourself."

THIRTY-FIVE

Iris leads me down a different hallway, and I get a small tour of the house. Despite its massive size, much of the interior feels surprisingly claustrophobic. The house isn't old, but it was designed to look that way. Lots of wood and stone, and the low ceilings make me feel like I have to duck through every doorway.

The kitchen, though, is surprisingly modern.

"We think the servants used this kitchen, and that's why it looks nothing like the rest of the house. Function over form, I guess," Iris says, anticipating my next weird question.

Three large stainless steel refrigerators line the far wall. Next to them is a commercial stove with a dozen burners, and the kitchen island is surrounded by shiny aluminum stools.

"We only use the fridge on the left," Iris says as she pulls out a stool and sits at the kitchen island.

"Cool, thanks," I say as I make my way to the fridge.

"Hey! Watch where you're walking!"

I jump back and realize I've almost stepped on a very,

very small man standing in front of the fridge. He must be less than six inches tall, roughly the size of an action figure. If he hadn't spoken, I would have thought he was a large mouse.

"I'm sorry. I, um, didn't see you there," I blurt out while my brain tries to comprehend what I'm looking at.

"Oh, really? You didn't see me? I'm five inches tall, of course you didn't see me! That's why you gotta keep a better eye out. Yeesh."

The incredibly small man flips me off and exits the kitchen. Much to my surprise, he has no trouble moving the swinging kitchen door despite it being ten times his size.

"Sorry about that. That's Julio. He's actually really nice, but if you catch him in a bad mood, it's best to stay out of his way," Iris tells me.

"Let me guess, he has the ability to shrink?"

"He *had* the ability to shrink. Unfortunately, he doesn't have the ability to return to his regular size."

"So, he's stuck like that?"

"For now. He's been working with a few others in the house to return to his normal size, but they've hit a dead end."

"That's gotta suck."

"He tries to stay optimistic. It's not all bad. He's retained his strength so, pound for pound, he's incredibly strong. It's helped him out more than a few times, mostly with birds. He stays inside the house now, especially with the temperature dropping and the woodland creatures desperate for food."

"Yikes, I hadn't even thought about that."

"You should see his room. That place is decked out like Barbie's Dream House on steroids. He has his own house, pool, roller coaster, racecar track-you name it. It's much cheaper to entertain yourself when you can furnish your entire place using a toy store."

I find milk in the fridge and cereal in a cabinet. I pour myself a bowl, and Iris pulls out a stool, gesturing for me to sit with her.

"What kind of trouble have you gotten yourself into?" Iris asks.

"Who said I'm in trouble?"

"You were at your brother's apartment on a school night, you nearly got yourself killed trying to land an airplane, and your metabands look like they're about to give out. I doubt I'm going out on a limb in assuming you're in trouble."

I sigh. It's no use keeping secrets from Iris. She has the uncanny ability to see right through any facade I put up. I start from the beginning and tell her everything, filling in any gaps in information with my best guesses. She listens intently and doesn't make dumb jokes every five seconds, like I would have if the roles were reversed.

"Wow, good job making so many enemies inside a week," she says.

"Tell me about it. I just tried to do the right thing. If I knew everyone would hate me for it, maybe I would have acted differently."

"I don't buy that."

"What do you mean?"

"I don't buy that you'd do things differently. Are you telling me you wouldn't have taken the nuclear core out of the reactor, even if it meant sacrificing workers?"

"I don't know. People said they knew the risks of their job. No one wanted those people to die, but I made a huge area completely uninhabitable. What about everyone who has to find a new job and move out of their home? Did I have the right to decide that for them?"

"No, you didn't, but you were faced with a problem few people will ever have to deal with. It's easy to look back and accept how things could have turned out if you'd never shown up. But you did show up, and you did what you thought was right. You weren't willing to trade human lives, and that's always the right call."

"I've killed before."

"I know. I have too. It's unavoidable in what we do. I wish that wasn't the case, but it is. I think about it all the time. It's the one thing I wish I could go back and change. In every instance, though, it was the only option I could see.

"There's a difference between taking a life when you have no choice and putting a price on the lives of innocent people. We don't sacrifice innocent lives-ever. We do everything we can to save people, no matter who they are or what they've done. It's the only responsible way to use the powers we have. If we believe we have the right to decide who deserves to live or die, how are we any different from the people we fight against?"

"You're talking about Kyle, or Judgment, rather."

"He thinks he knows better than anyone else how the world should be run. That never leads to anything good."

"How did you get to be so smart?"

Iris smirks. "I'm not smart. I've just had a lot of time to think about these things. It's one perk of being the daughter of a murderous psychopath."

It's quiet. Iris rarely talks about her father, the man who killed my parents, Jones. I'm not sure how to respond.

"Sorry to bring that up," she says, breaking the silence.

"No, it's okay. I know it's not easy to think about him."

"No, it's not."

More silence.

"If it's any consolation," I say, "I recently found out my dad might not be the hero I thought he was."

"What do you mean?"

"Kyle told me a story about a metahuman who crashed into an apartment building in Kaldonia. A lot of people died. Then the meta just flew away. It's why he hates metahumans. He said the metahuman was The Governor."

Iris pauses to think, then asks, "Do you believe him?"

"I don't know what to think. I never heard about that incident before, but so many things happened outside the US we never heard about back then. I could see the fire in his eyes when he told me about it. True or not, he believes it. I don't think he knows The Governor was my dad. If he did, he wouldn't have let me leave in one piece."

"Have you asked Midnight?"

"I hesitated to ask when I first found out, and he's been off the grid ever since. I haven't told Derrick either. They could get to the bottom of this pretty fast, but what if it's true?"

"It won't change who you are. I've grappled with that for a long time myself, but it's the truth. You're not condemned to repeat someone else's mistakes. For what it's worth, I don't think it's true. Your father was a good man."

"How can you say my dad was a good man when he killed yours?"

"Our fathers were friends before Jones's mind was broken. I know The Governor didn't make the decision to kill him lightly. If he had, he would have done it years earlier. You know better than I do how he's criticized to this day for not killing Jones sooner, before so many others died. Ultimately your father sacrificed himself to stop him. That doesn't sound like someone who would run from responsibility."

Iris's words make me feel like I can breathe for the first time since Kyle told me his story. I don't know if she's right, but it gives me hope.

"Thanks, Iris."

"Don't mention it."

"So, since you're handing out advice so freely, what should I do now?" I ask.

"Well I think you should rest. If those metabands still work, they'll need a chance to recharge."

"I was letting them recharge, but then someone flew over my brother's apartment, and I had to follow."

Iris smiles again. "Oh, now you're blaming this one on me? I didn't tell you to follow me. You're just nosey. You should learn how to mind your own business."

I laugh. "Okay, that's fair."

"All joking aside, you need rest. There's nothing more you can do tonight. Gaining abilities clouds a person's judgment like nothing else—we've both seen that—but sometimes, people move past it. Maybe Kyle will be one of those people.

"You should talk to him. Not as Omni, but as Connor. Don't go in there ready to punch him into the stratosphere. Talk to him the way Midnight talked to you when you found your metabands."

"Midnight strapped me to a table and threatened to torture me if I didn't tell him who I was."

"Ah, he wasn't really going to torture you. That was just a negotiating tactic."

"Did he tell you that?"

"No. Actually I forgot he did that. Nevertheless, talk to Kyle. If he wanted the power of a metahuman so badly, maybe you can help him understand what having that power means."

"Okay."

"But I'd probably make sure your metabands are working before you see him. Just in case."

THIRTY-SIX

I finish eating my cereal and feel much better with something in my stomach. Iris says she has some work to do, but directs me to an empty bedroom I can use on the second floor.

It's harder to find than I expected since this house has dozens of bedrooms. While searching, I hear strange noises coming from behind closed doors, and I'm extra cautious about opening any door until I'm sure I have the right room.

I eventually find it and realize it's the first time in months I have a room all to myself. Even before moving to the academy, I rarely had my own room with Derrick and me moving around a lot.

This reminds me that I should message Derrick and let him know I'm okay. The fact I haven't received any panicked texts yet means he must still be at the office.

I keep the message short. The more information I give him the more questions he'll ask. Plus, Iris swore me to secrecy, and few people would be more interested in this house than Derrick.

With the text sent, my responsibilities for the day are done.

I fall asleep before my head even hits the pillow.

THE SUNLIGHT COMING in through the window wakes me up early the next morning. I get up to close the blinds, hoping to catch more sleep, but the glare from the snow outside nearly blinds me. I pull the shades closed and wait for my eyes to adjust to the darkness, but it's no use. I lie back in bed and stare at the ceiling. There's no way I'm falling back asleep now.

I grab my phone off the nightstand and check to see if Derrick messaged me back. I hesitate, expecting him to be pissed at me, but decide I'm just avoiding the inevitable.

The first notification is indeed from Derrick. To my surprise, he's cool with what little information I gave him about my whereabouts. Maybe he's finally starting to relax now that I've been living out of the house for a few months. The only hint of worry is from him telling me to "be careful."

The next notification is from Midnight.

He's never been verbose, especially when texting, but after not hearing from him for so long, this one spurs me into action.

I jump out of bed and rush to grab my sneakers from the other side of the room. I return to the bedside to take my metabands off the nightstand. I examine them. The charred areas seem fainter than they were last night, but it's hard to tell. It doesn't matter.

I place the metabands on my wrists and look at my phone to make sure I didn't misread the message.

I didn't.
It's a set of GPS coordinates and one word:
Help.

THIRTY-SEVEN

As I clamor down the stairs, I consider looking for Iris to tell her. Whatever trouble Midnight's in, considering the state of my metabands, I could use the backup.

The problem is, I have no idea where to find her in the mansion. She could be anywhere.

I call out her name, but no one answers.

I glance at my phone and Midnight's four letter message. Just looking at it fills me with dread. He's never asked for help. All of this would be easier if Iris had taken Midnight up on his offer to use a communicator.

Hell, all this would be easier if Iris would just carry a phone on her.

There's no use thinking about this now. If Midnight needs help there's no time to spare.

I run out of the house and into the early morning light. The metabands around my wrists crackle with energy.

All I can do is hope I've given them enough time to recharge.

I bring my metabands together and activate them. Arcs of electricity connect the pair before they make contact.

The energy flows through my body uncomfortably, like it's too much to handle, but I clench my fists and take it.

The energy surge smoothes out, and the Omni suit pours over my body.

Ideally, I'd take a few minutes to kick the tires before taking off into the air, but I don't have time for that.

Besides, they feel *somewhat* all right. Not normal, but not too weird, I guess?

No more second-guessing myself. Either I'm doing this or I'm not.

I reach for my hip and the suit retracts to allow access to the pocket where I store my phone. I tap on the coordinates Midnight sent me, and they open inside the maps app.

The location is on the outskirts of Bay View City, just south of me. I zoom in to take a better look before I'm up in the air. Looks like it's an industrial area, maybe a shipping port. I memorize the area as best I can before return the phone to my pocket.

I crane my head back, looking skyward and hope this works.

I will myself to take to the air. There's a delay, then suddenly I'm flying, gaining altitude fast. The massive house below is the size of an ant.

My powers feel intact, but I'm having trouble controlling them.

With great effort, I point myself toward Bay View City. Again there's a delay before I take off like a rocket.

I try to keep my trajectory straight, but I'm flying too fast.

Signs of civilization appear below. The suburbs surrounding the city grow denser. I'm already getting close.

With the ocean on the horizon, it's time to concentrate on decelerating. It takes concentration, but I slow myself to crawl. I try to regain my momentum, but it feels impossible. Then, out of nowhere, I'm speeding through the air again. My powers are frustratingly difficult to control.

I spot the industrial area I'm looking for ahead. Afraid I'll overshoot it, I gather my concentration and stop trying to fly. For the first time today, my metabands listen to me.

I plummet from the sky, but I'm close enough to the docks to let gravity carry me the rest of the way. I pull my arms to my sides to make myself as aerodynamic as a missile.

The wind whistles past my ears as I pick up speed. The area matches what I found on the map. There's a large freighter leaving the dock and heading out to sea. The timing can't be coincidental, but I head toward the docks first. Better to stake out the situation before jumping in headfirst.

With my sights locked on an open area, I spread myself out to increase my surface area and reduce my speed.

If it's working, I don't notice.

The ground is growing closer by the second, and I can't slow down.

I'm coming in hot.

The brilliant idea to tuck and roll occurs to me half of a second too late.

I try anyway and wind up skidding across the dock on my back. I'm flailing my hands, desperate to grab onto something, anything, to stop my momentum.

After an eternity of sliding, I claw my right hand onto the side of a huge metal shipping container. Without other containers stacked on top to weigh it down, all I manage to do is drag it with me.

This isn't my day.

I maneuver myself toward a narrow gap between

containers. I slide through the gap, and the container I'm dragging gets stuck, bringing my slide to a stop.

I rise onto my feet, feeling aches and pains, and scan my surroundings. I'm relieved no one saw that truly embarrassing display, but then I worry I landed in the wrong place.

I walk to the water's edge and see I'm in the right place.

The lifeless bodies of five workers are strewn across the dock. I approach the one closest to me for further inspection, even though I don't want to.

There's a bullet wound in his chest. Based on the size of the wound, and from what Midnight's taught me, he was shot at close range. The next two bodies are lying on their stomachs, gunshot wounds in their backs.

You don't need to be a CSI to figure out they were shot as they ran away.

None of the bodies have any weapons on them, but the badges on their uniforms match the logo printed on the sides of the shipping containers.

This isn't a black market deal gone wrong. This is the cold-blooded murder of people who were in the wrong place at the wrong time.

I feel sick.

I've seen the aftermath of more violence than most people my age, and it still gets to me, especially when innocent people are slaughtered like this.

The anger I'm feeling has to be compartmentalized. It may be useful later, but it won't help me now.

Question is: Where's Midnight?

My suit retracts, and I pull my phone out of my pocket.

The coordinates have changed.

I tap them to bring up the map. There's a flashing red

dot that wasn't there a moment ago. Midnight's transmitter is back on and moving away from the dock.

Midnight is on the freighter, and I'm willing to bet whoever caused this carnage is onboard too.

Not trusting my ability to fly, or my ability to land on a moving target, I consider my options. There's really only one way onto that ship.

I take a few steps back and measure the distance. I can't push myself too hard. With the way my powers are acting, I could easily overshoot my target, but I don't want to undershoot it either.

I run as fast as I can until I reach the end of the pier. Then I leap.

I time the jump right, and sail straight for the departing ship.

A crew member on the deck spots me. We make eye contact a second before I collide with him. His machine gun skitters across the deck.

Another gunman runs out from behind a container and points his weapon at me while yelling in a foreign language.

Even though I don't understand what he's saying, I assume it's something along the lines of, "Hey, guys! He's over here!"

More gunmen hurry toward me from every direction. Guess I was right.

A few weeks ago, I would have barely broken a sweat fighting these guys, but I can't rely on the whole bulletproof thing today.

Better to rely on speed.

I lunge at the closest gunman and rip the gun from his hands. A front kick to the chest sends him flying across the deck and into a stack of steel containers. He won't be getting up anytime soon.

A hail of bullets flies past my head like a pack of angry bees. I rush toward their point of origin, bobbing and weaving faster than the muzzle of the gun can follow. I rip away the weapon of another gunman and throw it overboard.

Mad he almost shot me, I grab his collar and throw him overboard too.

The remaining gunmen surround me. That might seem like a good idea, but now they can't fire at me without the risk of hitting one of their comrades.

I run a circle around them, grabbing firearms as I pass before they grow confident enough to take a shot. A series of punches and kicks sends them either overboard or clear across the deck and into a growing pile of unconscious bodies.

With the immediate threat dealt with, I approach the one semiconscious gunman. He struggles onto his feet and draws a knife from his boot.

"Really?" I ask.

He lunges at me with a wild slash. I might not be bulletproof, but if that landing didn't kill me, I know I can handle a knife.

On his second attempt to slash me, I grab the knife and throw it into the ocean. Clutching his collar, I push him against a container.

"Who are you and what are you transporting?" I scream inches from his face.

He struggles against my grip, refusing to answer. Then a shot rings out, and the man goes limp.

Behind me, the shooter has his revolver pointed at my center mass. His expression is calm. The fact he missed me and killed his colleague doesn't seem to be weighing on his conscience.

It's time to uncork that anger I have bottled up.

He gets off a second shot quicker than I estimated. The bullet hits me in the chest, and I stagger backward.

It feels like a bull hit me while running at full speed. I touch my chest, expecting a gaping wound, but find the flattened bullet.

I've been shot before, but it never hurt like this.

The man fumbles to reload, giving me an opening. I walk up to him and wrap my gloved hand around his gun. His eyes widen, and I squeeze his hand still firmly wrapped around the gun's handle.

He howls in pain as the tiny bones inside his fingers snap one at a time.

Then I squeeze harder.

"You were going to kill me, huh? You already killed your friend over there, but that doesn't bother you. Tell me, how many of the dockworkers are the result of your handiwork?" I growl through gritted teeth.

He falls to his knees, pleading for me to let him go, but it only makes me want to squeeze harder.

"Where's Midnight?" I shout.

He doesn't answer. Tears stream down his face.

"If he's dead, you're going to wish you were too!"

His eyes roll back in his head. He's passing out from the pain.

"Stop!" a gruff voice shouts.

I relax my grip and look up, expecting shots to follow, but it wasn't a gunman who shouted.

It's Midnight.

He's not wearing his uniform, and he looks like he's been through hell.

But he's alive.

THIRTY-EIGHT

"What are you doing here? Where have you been? Why weren't you answering anyone's communications?"

"Give me a minute, kid."

I'm trailing behind Midnight as he struggles up the metal staircase to the bridge of the freighter. He's wearing jeans and a t-shirt along with multiple injuries to his arms and face. He pulls open the door and heads inside without waiting for me.

Typical. I follow behind, half expecting another fight, but the bridge is deserted.

"Um, who's piloting the ship?" I ask.

"I'd guess one of the guys you knocked out back there. It's not important. The ship's autopilot does most of the work. Besides, a ship this size usually gets the right of way."

Midnight rummages through a first aid station attached to the wall. He pulls out gauze and antiseptic ointment, then sits down to tend to his wounds.

"What happened back there?" Midnight asks as he unwinds the roll of gauze. "You looked like you were about to kill that man."

"Of course not. I mean, I wanted to, but I wouldn't have."

Midnight stops and studies my face the way he does when he thinks I'm lying. "Why did you want to?"

"I don't know. I was angry. They killed those dockworkers, and I thought they might have killed you."

"They tried." He wraps up a large gash across his right forearm. "I'm pretty sure they killed those men to draw me out."

"They knew you were here?"

Midnight nods. "I've been undercover, working on the ship. Somehow, they figured out one of us wasn't who he claimed to be, and they started looking for a mole. That's why I was out of communication. Any radio waves transmitted or received on the ship would have been easy to detect out on the open ocean where there's little interference."

"You've been working on a shipping freighter? How did you get on board?"

"I poisoned a crew member's dinner the night before they were scheduled to leave. Then I made sure I was in the right place at the right time the next morning when they were desperate for an extra set of hands."

"You're mad at me for wanting to hurt a guy I thought had killed you, and meanwhile, you're out there poisoning guys?"

"Not all poisons are deadly. He was good as new less than twenty-four hours after the ship left port."

"And they didn't suspect the mole was the new guy?"

"I was high on the suspect list, but I stuck to my story right up until they started executing other suspects."

"Why didn't they kill you first?"

Midnight smiles. "I was the cook. A damn good one too.

Killing me would mean eating peanut butter and crackers for dinner. No one wants that, so they convinced themselves someone else was guilty. Speaking of which, come on. I've got to go secure the crew."

Wincing, Midnight rises from his seat and walks back out the door. I glance around the bridge at all the dials and controls I don't understand, still worried the ship might crash without someone at the wheel.

I have no idea how any of this works so I'll just have to trust him.

Outside the cabin, Midnight already has one crew member hogtied and is working on the second. This is what he meant by *securing* them.

"Where did the ship depart?" I ask.

"Kaldonia."

"Are you serious?"

"Yes."

"What the hell were you doing there?"

"Following a lead."

I take a length of rope from a pile on the deck and walk over to an unconscious crewman. Before I can lay a hand on him, Midnight snatches it away from me.

"I appreciate you trying to help, but let me do it since I'll just have to do it again anyway."

I'd be angry if he wasn't right.

"So, why are you so interested in this ship? What is it hauling?"

"Cheap Kaldonian fabric, but its cover. The important thing is what we were sent here to bring back."

"Which is?"

"Deactivated metabands from the same black market shipment we stopped on the bridge last week. Kaldonia is importing them be combined with magtonium, but once they knew there was a mole onboard, the shipment was redirected. It's not what you, or anyone else, thinks it is," he says.

"What do you mean?"

Midnight pauses midway through tying up another crewman, contemplating how to explain it, but he shakes his head and returns to tying up the crewman. "I can't say. Not yet."

"Not yet? What does that mean? Is this a future thing? Can you not tell me because it might affect the timeline?"

There's one rule above all of Midnight's other rules, and that's not to ask about the future. He's told me repeatedly to forget I even know that's where he's from since it's not something he can talk about, but my question just blurts itself out. I'm surprised when he doesn't immediately reprimand me for even asking.

"The timeline's already been affected. None of this was ever supposed to happen the way it has. The future I'm from doesn't exist anymore, but that doesn't mean things can't get worse. Things can always get worse. That's what I'm trying to prevent. I know you're curious, but this is too important."

I don't press the issue. When Midnight goes out of his way to be nice, it usually means whatever he's talking about is serious.

"Tell me what you already know," Midnight says.

"Everything I know comes from Kyle Toslov."

"Hmm. Not the most reliable source."

"I take it that means you saw what happened with the plane last night?"

"There's a shortwave radio in the kitchen. I heard a brief synopsis. The media doesn't know what to make of him."

"I don't think anyone knows what to make of him, but that hasn't stopped people from rallying behind him."

"That's potentially dangerous."

"Duh."

Midnight glares at me. I forgot that saying *duh* is also at the top of the list of things he's asked me not to do around him.

"Um, so is there anything Kyle hasn't told me that you can?"

"It's not what he hasn't told you; it's what he doesn't know. He's smart, very smart, but his level of hubris is extremely troubling. No one else in his home country knows how to work with magtonium the way he does, but that doesn't mean he understands it. Not even close. But he knows enough to make himself very dangerous. I assume he told you there's AI embedded in the magtonium he's experimenting with?"

"He did, but I don't really understand it."

"Then that makes two of you. Hopefully, that's all you have in common," he says with a glower.

"Earlier, with that crew member, that was just, I don't know. I was scared. You know that's not me."

Midnight finishes tying up the last crew member and leans against a container. "It's fine to get scared. I get scared too. It's part of what we do. You'd have to be a psychopath not to be scared in life and death situations, and I can guarantee Kyle is scared too. But once you let that fear make decisions for you? That's a hard road to come back from."

"Do you think Kyle can?"

"I'm not sure."

"What now?"

"Now? Now I suggest you rest those things." Midnight points at my metabands.

"Do you know what's going on with them?"

"No, I don't, and I'm not just saying that to protect the timeline. I genuinely have not seen a pair of metabands damaged quite like that before."

"Lucky me."

"They're self-healing, as you know, but they might be damaged beyond their ability to fully restore themselves. That doesn't mean they're destined to become non-functional, but you might have to adjust."

"How can I adjust to a pair of unreliable metabands?"

"By changing your expectations. You'll have to give them more time to recharge. It also means no more biting off more than you can chew. That's how you got into this predicament in the first place. You'll have to be careful about the battles you choose from here on out, because judging by their appearance, you shouldn't trust them to get you out of a tight spot anymore."

"Thanks for the depressing news."

"They're still better than what I've got," Midnight says, holding up his two bare wrists. "It sounds like you have a relationship with Kyle?"

"I was starting to, but that went south when he killed a man in cold blood."

Midnight exhales loudly through his nose and places a hand on my shoulder. "I know it won't be easy, but maybe there's a chance he'll listen to you. Everyone needs time to find their way. Just because he's done something horrible, it doesn't mean he can't change. Don't rely on your fists for this one. You can't count on them anyway."

"Okay, I'll try. And what are you going to do?"

"My work isn't done. I have a lot of questions for my sleeping beauties here. After that, I'm heading back to Kaldonia to finish up some business."

"You think they'll just let this ship back in, no questions asked?"

"Of course not. There's a submersible on autopilot on its way to me. I'll use that to get into the country undetected. It has one or two things on board that'll come in handy, including a change of clothes."

"Didn't take a suit onboard with you?"

"Too risky. They searched our belongings thoroughly. Even I would have had a hard time hiding a suit in such close quarters."

"Makes sense."

"You'd better get going before we're too far from the shore. I don't want you draining those things more than you have to."

"Yeah, you're right."

"I'll have my communicator back once the submersible arrives, but I'll need to be careful using it inside the Kaldonian border. With that said, if you need me, call. I'll do my best to help. Otherwise, please be careful."

I look at the sky and am about to leap, but I hesitate.

"Everything all right?" Midnight asks.

"Yeah... No, actually."

Midnight cocks his head.

"It's something Kyle told me about my dad—or about The Governor. Do you know anything about him crashing into Kaldonia during a fight?"

Midnight stares into the distance, thinking. "Why?"

"Kyle told me The Governor crashed into an apartment building in Kaldonia. Three hundred and seventeen people died, but The Governor did nothing."

Midnight sighs. "Did I ever tell you about the time your dad appeared at the grand opening of a shopping mall?"

"He did?"

"It wasn't something he was proud of."

"I never knew he did any kind of publicity stunts. Everything I heard about The Governor before I knew he was my dad was that he avoided that kind of stuff, even though there was a lot of money being thrown around then."

"He did, and there was. A month earlier, he'd fought a new metahuman. It was a typical new metahuman with bad intentions. The guy was trying to rob a bank if I remember correctly. Your father showed up, and in a panic, the metahuman fired an energy blast at your dad. The Governor ducked, not thinking about what was behind him. The blast hit a customer and vaporized him."

"Oh man."

"It put your dad in a dark place for a long time. The victim had a wife and a newborn daughter. It wasn't your dad's fault, and even with his powers, a blast like that could have killed him at close range. Still, he never forgave himself.

"When he was approached about the mall opening, they offered him enough money to support the widow and her daughter for life, and he didn't hesitate to accept even though he found it humiliating. The money went into a private trust with the stipulation the woman could never find out where the money came from. It was the only way he saw to try to make things right."

"I never heard that story before."

"Not many knew about it. He'd be mad at me for even telling you about it."

"So, Kyle's story isn't true?"

"I know the incident Kyle's referring to, but I never heard anyone pin the blame on The Governor. Usually the specifics aren't mentioned to avoid exposing the lie underneath. The apartment building collapsed due to sloppy construction. Government officials were bribed to pass inspection. Those bribes went right into Mikah Akulov's pocket. If the people had known, there would have been riots in the street. Instead, Akulov blamed a metahuman, killing two birds with one stone. He gave the people of Kaldonia a common enemy while hiding the truth."

"I can't tell you how much of a relief that is to hear."

"Your father was a good man, Connor. The best I've ever known, metahuman or not. He wasn't perfect, and he couldn't always save everybody, but it was what he did in those situations that made him a true hero."

THIRTY-NINE

I launch into the air and head back toward shore. I'll have to take it low and slow to make sure these metabands don't peter out before I make it back onto dry land. I'm a decent swimmer, but I can barely see the coastline from here. I really don't want to have to call Midnight and ask him to come and pluck me out of the ocean.

The air is calm, and without buildings to worry about, I can skim low over the ocean. Within a few moments, the coast is close enough and I push myself higher.

I think about the gunman on the ship and ask myself what I would have done to him if Midnight had been killed. Would I have lost control? It's a terrifying thought, but one I have to consider. I don't ever want to be in a situation where I don't trust myself again.

I guess Kyle and I are more alike than I thought. If I'm having trouble controlling my emotions, why am I surprised Kyle is too? I've been at this a lot longer than him.

I think back to the beginning, when Midnight found me. No one had seen a metahuman in a decade. He didn't know what to make of me and treated me like a threat, but in time he became a mentor.

It's easy to imagine how bad things could have gone for me if Midnight hadn't shown up when he did. I had no idea how to control my powers, and the responsibility they came with was lost on me. Kyle's likely going through the same thing.

Out of nowhere, I lose altitude and skim the ocean's surface. I snap my attention back to flying and regain my previous elevation. I can't let my mind wander too far in my current state. My abilities are taking more focus than they used to.

I swipe my metabands to bring up their power indicator. I'm running low, and I'll have to find a place to land soon.

FORTY

Kyle's apartment building stands out against the rest of the landscape. Flying low, I spot a deserted park to land in. I take one last look around to make sure the coast is clear then descend.

As soon as my feet touch the ground, I click my metabands together to power down. There isn't the same electric jolt I experienced the last few times. It's hard to explain, but my metabands feel tired.

It seems strange to think about them that way, but considering our bond, it shouldn't be surprising. When I have them on and activated, they sharpen every single one of my senses on top of the abilities they grant, so why wouldn't I be able to sense their condition too?

I shift the metabands out of this reality to hide them. This is risky, but I want to appear as unthreatening as possible. Having my metabands ready to activate at a moment's notice in my hoodie pockets wouldn't signal "unthreatening." Neither would having them on my wrists.

As I approach the apartment building, I give my sweatshirt a quick sniff test. I've been wearing the same clothes since yesterday, but I smell fine. Add the power to eliminate B.O. to my list of underrated abilities.

I get the sense something's wrong. My metabands aren't on my wrists, so it's not from them. It's just good old-fashioned human sixth sense.

It feels too quiet.

I enter the building and my feeling is confirmed. There's no one behind the front desk, and the chair is tipped over. The elevator is parked on the ground floor, its doors stuck open. I opt to take the stairs.

On Kyle's floor, I find his door wide open. I hurry into his apartment.

A chill runs down my spine.

Sarah's new exosuit is lying face down on the floor.

I run over, not sure if she's inside or not. I grab an arm and flip the exosuit onto its back.

"Sarah!"

Her eyes are closed, and blood is smeared across her forehead. I try to shake her, but the suit is too heavy. My heart is racing as I keep yelling her name. I check her suit for any clues as to how it got so damaged.

Her eyes flutter open.

"Stay still. You're okay," I say.

I pull out my cell phone and tap the screen, but nothing happens. Dammit. I didn't plug it in last night and the battery is dead.

"Connor," Sarah says hoarsely.

"I'm here."

She moves the exosuit's massive arm to support herself, but it slips and she collapses back onto the floor.

"Easy, Sarah. I'll go get help. Stay still in case something's broken."

I look around Kyle's apartment for a phone. I don't see

one, but I notice a huge hole in the wall where a window used to be.

I look down at Sarah and notice something else. The metaband that's normally embedded in the chest of the suit, the one that belonged to Midnight, is gone, and the area is heavily damaged. It was removed by force.

"Who did this?" I ask.

"Kyle."

I knew the answer the second I walked into the apartment, but I had to hear it from her to know for sure.

"Why did he do this?"

Sarah starts to struggle again.

"Please, don't try to get up."

"I'm not."

She reaches across her body to the gauntlet on her right forearm and presses a few buttons. There's a loud release of pressure, and parts of the suit pop open. Two interlocking pieces are twisted, causing problems with the internal mechanisms. Sarah pushes against them, anxious to get out of the suit.

"Hold on, hold on," I say as I rematerialize the metabands around my wrists and bring them together to activate, but it doesn't work.

Sarah squints in confusion.

"Are those okay?" She asks as she continues to grapple with the chest plate.

"Not really."

I bring the metabands together again. They show signs of life, like a car's engine reluctantly turning over after multiple attempts.

To save energy, I don't deploy the Omni suit.

Feeling stronger, I wrap my fingers around the chest pieces refusing to budge and pull them apart.

Sarah helps pushing them aside and begins crawling out of the suit. I offer her a hand, making sure she takes it slow in case she's injured.

Once she's out, she raises a sleeve to wipe away the blood from the small cut on her forehead. She otherwise looks okay. I help her over to one of the chairs near the kitchen counter and pour her a glass of water from the kitchen sink.

"Thanks," she says, still catching her breath.

"What happened?" I ask.

"I don't remember it all. I came here to talk with Kyle. I wanted to confront him about what he's been doing, but he wasn't himself. He was at first, but then he changed. He was angry. It started to build the moment I asked about the plane crash. He didn't want to talk about it, but then he wouldn't stop talking about it. He went on and on about how it had been the right thing to do. How it was necessary if we didn't want the entire galaxy overrun by metahumans. It didn't make sense, and he was scaring me."

"Did you tell him that?"

"I did. I'd hoped it'd deescalate the situation, but he just got more aggressive."

"Angrier?"

"No, that's just it. He was almost giddy. I told him he was scaring me, and he started grinning ear-to-ear. Of course, that just frightened me even more."

"Is that when you went for your suit?"

"No, I wasn't even thinking about the suit. I was nervous, but I didn't think Kyle would ever do anything violent. I only had the suit with me because I was bringing it to the robotics lab for some repairs later today when nobody would be there."

"Then what happened?"

"That's the part I don't remember. The last thing I remember is Kyle giving me this sinister smile, and then I woke up with you here. I don't even remember putting the suit on."

I look around the apartment again, trying to piece together the events.

"Does the suit have an automatic defense feature?"

"There are a few fail-safes that prevent it from damaging itself or hurting me, but most of those have been disabled."

"Midnight disabled them?"

"No, I did. They felt constricting. Once I was confident using the suit, I turned them off. I only touched the code I understood. Anything pertaining to the suit's functions I wasn't familiar with, I left alone."

"Hmm. Knowing Midnight, there are likely emergency safety protocols embedded in there. The suit must have detected you were in danger and activated. Honestly, it makes more sense that Midnight let you keep the suit if he knew it could protect you in an emergency."

"You're saying he only gave me the suit as protection?"

"Not at all. There are easier ways to protect someone than giving them high-tech exo-armor, but it might have been a factor. He wouldn't have parted with his sole metaband unless he knew it could save your life someday. Looks like that day was today."

"Where's the metaband? Oh no..." Sarah goes quiet.

"What is it?"

"I just remembered. I regained consciousness. I could see him, Kyle, but he's wasn't Kyle anymore. He was Judgment. He was wrapped in magtonium and reaching for me. I felt him ripping the metaband out of my chest. The suit tried to fight it. It tried waking me up to stop him, but I couldn't stay awake."

I examine the exosuit more closely. There's a dent in the back of the helmet.

"This must be where he hit you and knocked you unconscious. The suit must have tried to protect you when he came up from behind. We should get you to a hospital in case you have a concussion. I'll go downstairs and use the phone at the front desk to call for an ambulance. You stay here and try not to move too much. Whatever you do, don't fall asleep."

I pull my sleeves down over the metabands to hide them from any nosy neighbors and head to the door.

"There's one more thing," Sarah says.

I stop in my tracks.

"The metaband in the suit, the one that belonged to Midnight, after Kyle pulled it out of my chest, he wrapped his hands around it and consumed it. When he was done there was nothing left."

FORTY-ONE

"An ambulance is on its way," I announce as I walk into Kyle's apartment.

Sarah is sitting at the dining room table hunched over something. The large television taking up the living room wall is tuned to news coverage of the aftermath of yesterday's plane crash.

"What are you doing? You should stay still until the ambulance gets here," I say.

"You also told me not to fall asleep. I have to do something to keep my mind active."

"What is that?"

She's working on something that looks vaguely like a ping-pong paddle, but a bunch of wires lead from the handle to a connector plugged into Sarah's laptop.

"It's a diagnostic wand. It's what Kyle used to program the magtonium nanotech."

"I think it's a little late for that to be of much use."

"That's because you're not thinking creatively, Connor."

"Huh?"

"When Kyle was working on this stuff, he didn't get it right the first time. It took multiple iterations. He couldn't work on the nanotech code while it was active. He had to work on his laptop and transfer the data over each time he made changes. This weird looking thing is how he did it. He couldn't just plug the magtonium into a USB port to update the code. He had to create a way to transmit the code wirelessly."

"Can we use it to reprogram the nanotech?"

"I don't know if we can reprogram it while it's active. I don't have access to his codebase, and even if I did, it would take days before I could make heads or tails of it. But maybe we can wipe the magtonium's memory. That wouldn't require rewriting or understanding the code. It'd be like ripping a computer's plug out of the wall while it's still on. It would make the magtonium completely inert."

"That sounds like it could work. How long until you can get it working?"

"I'm working on it now. There are protections built in to prevent anyone from using it while the nanotech is active, but they're weak and only meant to prevent an accidental mishap. He never anticipated the device could be used this way intentionally. I have no way of knowing whether it'll work. This is very exotic technology, and I'm making a lot of guesses about how it works. This is more of a Hail Mary than a sure thing."

"It's better than nothing."

While Sarah works, I find a power adapter and plug in my phone.

A *Breaking News* graphic flashes on the television. It's an image I'm getting really tired of seeing. An anchor seated at a news desk appears on screen.

"Breaking news this afternoon as we're receiving reports

of violent metahuman activity near downtown Bay View City, close to the scene of the dramatic 747 landing. A number of metahumans have been aiding with the wreckage cleanup at the scene, and at this time, it is unclear if any of them are involved in the violence. We have our team on their way there and will have a live feed momentarily. Again, reports coming into our newsroom are that a potentially dangerous metahuman incident is occurring in downtown Bay View City at the site of last night's plane crash. We advise our viewers to stay away from this area until we have more information."

"Kyle?" Sarah asks.

"It has to be."

"Why there?"

"He's looking for metahumans."

I yank the cord out of my phone and pocket it before concentrating on activating the Omni suit. Sarah sees it slowly emerge from my metabands and stands up from her chair.

"Whoa, what the hell are you doing?"

"I'm going to talk with Kyle."

"Are you crazy? You told me I shouldn't be moving around, but you're going out there to fight with your glitchy, barely working metabands?"

"I'm going to talk, not fight."

"I'm not sure that's up to you."

"I have to do something."

"Metahumans are already down there. Let them handle it until you know what you're getting into."

"I can't just sit around while a bunch of people trying to help are potentially in danger. I know Kyle. I've been where he is. I can talk to him."

"Connor, please. Don't do this. You haven't seen him.

You don't know what he's become. I don't know if there's anything of Kyle left in there."

I look out through the missing window and see paramedics exiting an ambulance.

"Help is here. They'll check you out and make sure you're okay."

"I'm fine, but you're going to get yourself killed if you go out there!"

I walk over and grab the paddle Sarah was working on from the table. "Don't worry, I've got a ping-pong paddle to protect me," I say with a smile.

Sarah doesn't laugh or return the smile.

"I have to go."

Sarah turns her back to me, furious.

I pause, but my mind is already made up.

"I'm sorry."

It's the only thing I can think to say.

FORTY-TWO

I push myself harder than I should to get to Kyle faster. I can't take it slow when every second might mean more destruction. I can hear small explosions near the scene, and people are running to escape the chaos.

I will myself to slow down, but instead I come to a dead stop. I fall from the sky and tumble onto the pavement, narrowly missing a fleeing businessman who screams as I hit the pavement.

Judging from the noise and the fleeing people, Kyle is close, possibly right around the corner. As I hurry toward the source of the noise, a frightened man runs up to me. His eyes are wide and his clothes are in tatters.

I assume he needs my help and ask, "Are you okay?"

"Don't. Don't go over there. He's insane," he mutters.

"It's okay, I can handle it. Thank you, though."

As I brush past, he grabs my arm. "Omni, listen to me. I'm Maverick."

I look at him inquisitively. He doesn't look like Maverick, but I don't look like Omni without my metabands activated either.

"I don't know how I can prove it to you, but please, just believe me. He's too powerful. I don't know what's going on with your metabands, but you have to listen to me."

"I'm fine."

"I saw you just fall out of sky. I'm not kidding, Omni. He'll kill you. He only spared me because I gave him what he wanted and ran."

"What did he want?"

"My metabands."

"You gave him your metabands?"

"He said he'd kill me if I didn't—and he meant it. I watched him kill others. Fighting him is useless. If you go to him, he'll get what he wants: more metabands. That's why he came to the crash site. He knew there would be TV cameras here and lots of people. He wants to attract as many metahumans as he can. He wants to take their metabands and their power."

"I can't just leave. I have to talk to him."

After a slight pause, he says, "You think I'm a coward for giving him my metabands, don't you?"

I look into his eyes and see his deep shame. He's afraid too. Even though he's safe now, his pupils are dilated and his eyes are wild. He just got the scare of his life, and it will be some time before he can calm down.

"I don't think you're a coward," I say. "You did what you had to in order to survive. There's no shame in that."

He doesn't respond, looking shell-shocked, and I doubt my words offer much solace.

"I have to go," I say.

He's tried his best to stop me, and there's nothing more he can do. Without another word, he shuffles off down the street in a daze. I watch him for a moment, then I turn back to face the inevitable.

As I near the corner, most of the loud noises have stopped. Car alarms are going off and water is pouring out of a hydrant, but the explosions have ceased.

There's no point in using caution. I'm sure Judgment knows I'm coming.

I round the corner and find a scene of massive destruction.

Cars are overturned everywhere, and a few are on fire. Storefront windows are all blown out. Dust and smoke hang in the air, making it hard to take in the entire situation. I could adjust my vision to cut through it, but my powers are too low to even attempt it.

My priority is finding any survivors. After some debate, I briefly switch my vision to infrared to look for heat signatures. There aren't any.

That's when I see Judgment.

He's standing in the middle of the street with his back to me. The nanite based suit looks larger, striking a more imposing silhouette. Its edges are sharper, giving it a more sinister look. The red lines running through it are wider and brighter, the suit more red than black.

I approach with my arms outstretched to my sides.

I'm not here to fight.

Judgment is leaning over something, the red in the suit pulsing.

"I was wondering when you would finally show up," he says, his back still to me. His voice is deep and distorted, and I get the sense I'm no longer talking to just Kyle.

"My metabands aren't working so well these days," I say.

Judgment turns to me. He's holding a pair of metabands in his hands, although calling them hands isn't quite right. His fingers are closer to tendrils, and they're each wrapped tightly around the metabands. The metabands are glowing brightly and crumpling as the tendrils crush them.

"Did you know that metabands have different power levels?" he asks.

I take a few steps closer. "I never knew for sure, but I always thought they might. Some say the power level has more to do with the person using them, though."

"That's a factor, but after consuming nineteen pairs, I can tell there are indeed different power levels. The more powerful ones take longer to digest, but the result is worth the effort."

It's strange to hear Kyle's observations coming through Judgment's harsh, distorted voice, but it also confirms there's something left of him in there.

"Your metabands will be much easier to break down. They'll make a nice dessert, almost like an after-dinner mint, don't you think?" Judgment asks with an amused smile.

"Kyle, I know you're still in there. I know deep down you don't want to do this. It's the artificial intelligence that wants more power. That's what's driving you to do this."

Judgment laughs. "You think the AI is making me do this? The AI wants me to *stop*. It's worried I'm overloading it with power. This amount of magtonium was never meant to consume so many metabands in one sitting. I'm the one overriding *it*, not the other way around."

"Okay, then maybe you should listen to the AI," I say.

"No."

Blinding white light erupts from the metabands in Judgment's hands. When the light fades, I watch as the tendrils rip apart the metabands' remains and pull it into his suit.

Judgment throws his head back and unleashes a guttural scream as the red lines in the suit pulsate brightly.

After a few seconds, the lines return to their previous brightness. Judgment shakes his head like he's clearing cobwebs from his brain.

"That was a good one," he says.

"Please, Kyle—"

"There's no Kyle anymore, Omni. I am Judgment now."

I concentrate on my cowl and force it to recede to expose my face. "I'm not Omni, Kyle. I'm Connor. It's not too late to stop before more people get hurt."

"Are you threatening me?" The smile on his face suggests he hopes I am.

"No. There's not much I can do stop you, but eventually someone will. When they do, they won't offer you mercy."

"I hope they don't. Mercy is an overrated concept. It's why we're all in this mess. It's what cowards hide behind when they're unwilling to do what's right.

"I take no pleasure in killing. I allowed those willing to give up their metabands to leave. I could have taken their lives, but I deemed it unnecessary. However, I will not hesitate to kill when I need to. That's the difference between you and me."

"Why do you think you deserve that power?"

"See, that's your problem. You think too small. Why do I think I deserve that power? Who cares? How much time have you wasted thinking about these things when you could have been making a difference? No wonder Sarah wants nothing to do with you."

I take a deep breath and try not to let that comment get to me. He wants to get under my skin and goad me into a fight so he can take my metabands. I refuse to take the bait.

"I'd rather Sarah want nothing to do with me than

destroy something she cares about and leave her unconscious on the floor."

Judgment pauses to think about this.

"To each his own, I guess. Speaking of wasting time, you know I can only chat for so long before I'll have to take those poor excuses for metabands from you?"

"Why do you even want them if they're practically useless?"

"Because every bit counts."

"Is that what you'll keep telling yourself until that stuff wrapped around you blows up?"

"No, of course not. I merely need enough energy to stay powered indefinitely. I might need to jolt the battery from time to time, but I'd rather not do so in a state of desperation. In time, people will forgive what I've done today when they see what I can accomplish tomorrow.

"No matter how successful I am, however, there will always be idiots like you. I'm not naive enough to think otherwise. They'll bide their time, waiting until I'm weak or powered down to strike. History is littered with those who were defeated because they let their guards down. With enough metabands, I can make sure my guard will never be down.

"But enough procrastinating, Omni. Give me those metabands. It's the only way to atone for your mistakes. Otherwise, you'll be no different from him."

"Than who?" I ask, confident I know who he's referring to.

"Than the heartless monster who killed my friend."

"The Governor didn't kill your friend. He didn't kill anyone in Kaldonia. Your father's negligence caused those deaths. He blamed a metahuman because he was an easy scapegoat. Can't you see that? Haven't you ever wondered why no one else in the world outside of Kaldonia believes that story?"

The red lines in the magtonium suit burn brighter. Judgment's eyes are glowing red. Through clenched teeth, he says, "You lie! This is your last warning. Give me those metabands or I'll rip them from your corpse."

FORTY-THREE

The word *no* has barely left my mouth before the first blow comes. I wasn't expecting it considering the distance between us. I've forgot the nanites can stretch into any shape Kyle wants. That's how the punch managed to connect from over twenty feet away.

It's not the first punch that hurts, though. It's the layers of sheetrock, concrete, and glass that it propels me through. It feels like I'll never stop. My back breaks through layer after layer as I sail through the building. I crash through the outer wall, keep going, and smash into the building on the other side of the block, where the same process starts all over again.

I'm three blocks away before I hit a wall that's too hard to break through. I bounce off it and land in a crumpled heap on the street. I flip onto my stomach and try to stand, but my legs collapse under me.

There's no way I'll last in a fight against him. He's too strong. I concentrate on my suit and will it to retract from my pocket. I pull out the diagnostic wand Sarah reprogrammed. It's shattered and useless now. I drop the wand

and focus on willing my cowl over my face. Exposing my identity is the last thing I should be worried about, but old habits die hard.

My metabands are completely black.

I spit on the pavement and recoil in horror at the red splat on the ground. Even the reserve power in the bands can't protect me anymore.

As I stare at the small puddle of blood, a shadow falls over me and the entire street darkens. Judgment emerges through the side of a building across the street. Rubble and debris fall from the sky and bounce along the road. He's so powerful, he didn't even bother flying over the building.

He's simply pushed himself through it.

"Connor, is this worth dying for? Look at you. The metabands aren't doing anything anymore. Do you think the world will remember your bravery? Because I have news for you: They won't. Your name will become synonymous with prideful ignorance. You'll be little more than a cautionary tale used to convince others to give up their metabands if they do not want to suffer the same ignoble fate."

He's no longer calling me Omni. At first, I'm hopeful that means he's relating to me as a human being again, but then I realize he's calling me Connor as an insult. He's implying I'm so weak he doesn't consider me a metahuman anymore.

"Last chance, Connor," Judgment says as he descends from the sky.

I try to say *no* again, but I'm having trouble getting enough air into my lungs. I shake my head and even that hurts.

Judgment sighs.

And then he lunges.

He wraps one hand around my throat and lifts me onto

my feet. I can feel myself losing consciousness. He eases his grip before I can pass out.

His other hand goes for my wrists. I pathetically attempt to hide my hands behind my back.

Long black tendrils emerge from his hand and wrap around my back, bringing both hands forward. They dig into my skin since there's no gap between the band and my wrists. The pain is excruciating. With both my wrists now secured, he releases his grip around my throat.

"There, that's better, isn't it? I'm no sadist, Connor. I do not wish to cause you more pain than necessary."

More tendrils emerge from elsewhere on his suit and wrap around my metabands. They use the bloody trenches he's already dug into my wrists as a guide.

Judgment takes a deep breath.

"Yours are quite different from all the others, aren't they? I could tell right away. Even in their condition, I can feel the unique power within them."

I remain silent. I refuse to use my last words to explain to him why my metabands are different.

"You won't tell me more about them, will you? I suppose I'll have to figure it out myself once you're gone."

Energy leaves my body as the metabands grow darker. The pain intensifies, and then it's replaced with numbness. The small amount of energy left in the metabands is redirected to give me some comfort in my last moments.

"I'll let you in on a little secret, Connor, now that we're at the end," Judgment says. He leans in close and the mask recedes to let Kyle's face come through. He whispers, even though we're the only two souls for blocks. "I was going to kill you anyway. I know I said I take no joy in it. Hell, I even let the others go, didn't I? But you're different. Even without your metabands, I can tell you'll be a problem, won't you? Yeah, you will be. As soon as you handed these over, boom, I was going to end you right where you stood. So well played on calling my bluff. You bought yourself a few extra minutes of life. Although this is a more painful way to go than I intended. Sorry, but you wanted it this way."

Everything around me is fading.

"I'll tell you what, Connor. I've already drained all I can, and I'm curious to test the limits of a dying pair of metabands. Since you're such a fan of mercy, I'll offer it to you. You merely have to ask, and I'll give you a swift death just to prove there are no hard feelings, but you will have to indulge me. I'll need you to beg."

Judgment loosens his grip, and I fall to my knees.

"Ha! There we go, good. Now just say the words."

I struggle to lift my head and look him in the eye, but it's too difficult.

"Come on, ask for mercy and you'll have it."

My hands shake as I raise them in front of me. I lick my lips and try to speak, but nothing comes out.

Judgment eases his grip further. "Oh, my God, you're actually going to beg? Oh, wow. I knew this had to be painful, but wow. This is so much better than I'd hoped."

I lock eyes with Kyle. I've never seen him so happy. My mouth is wet with blood. I try to speak again, but the words won't come out.

"Come on, you can do it..." Kyle encourages.

I take a final deep breath and dig down for the last scrap of energy my body can summon before it gives up.

And I use it to bring my metabands together one last time.

FORTY-FOUR

There's darkness followed by a blinding white light. I assume the worst: That it didn't work.

That I'm dead.

It feels like I am floating in space and my body no longer exists.

Then slowly, the white light fades.

I look down at my wrists.

My metabands are gone, and in their place is the white light. The magtonium nanites surround the white light. They're being pulled into the light. It's happening so quickly the magtonium is a blur. A loud whooshing sound is drowning everything out.

Then it stops and there's silence.

I look up from my wrists and see I'm still on the same street. Looks like I'm alive.

Kyle is no longer in front of me, but there's a cloud of dust across the street. As the wind disperses it, I can make out the shape of a person.

I run over and find Kyle lying outside a shop's blown-out window. His magtonium suit is gone. There's no blood, but he's not moving. I grab him by his shoulders to prop him upright and place my fingers on his neck. I feel a faint pulse. He's alive.

I need help, but the street is barren. My phone probably didn't survive the blast, but I reach into my pocket anyway.

My eyes are off Kyle for an instant, but when I look back, he's staring right at me. Before I can react, he hits me across the right side of my face. My hand is still in my pocket, and I'm thrown off balance. I tumble onto the pavement, my face taking the brunt of the fall.

Kyle is already on top of me. He's punching me, his eyes wide and frantic. I put my hands up to block the blows, but it's no use. The punches are coming too fast from every direction. Kyle is screaming so loudly I can't make out what he's saying. It sounds like random words, but I catch a few like *kill* and *you*.

He stands and winds up to stomp on my chest. I close my eyes and put my hands out to block it, but his foot never lands. Kyle's frustrated rage morphs into a howling wail.

I open my eyes to see him cowering on the ground next to me, cradling his foot as he rocks back and forth. He's screaming in agony.

That's when I notice my forearm.

It's covered in red magtonium.

I brush at it, thinking it's leftover material from when I deactivated my metabands, but the material doesn't budge.

It's like it's glued to my skin.

Worried, I scramble onto my feet.

The material is spreading up my forearm, slowly at first and then rapidly. In an instant the magtonium has covered my entire body. The surface moves and shifts like liquid.

Kyle looks up from his foot, which is most likely broken, and rage again takes over. His jaw clenches, and his hands ball into fists. He struggles to stand and then sprints at me.

I instinctively put my hands up to block him. He takes a wild swing. The punch connects with my face, but I barely feel it.

Again, he lets out a pained yelp. The fingers of his hand are bloody and crooked.

"That's mine! Give it back. Now!" he yells and rushes at me again.

This time, he tries a kick me in the chest, but it's as ineffective as the punch.

Without warning, a huge rush of adrenaline courses through my system. I thought I was dying, but now my body feels overwhelmed.

Rage bubbles to the surface from deep in my gut. I thrust my hand out, grab Kyle by the throat, and lift him off the ground.

His pupils dilate, and he kicks and claws at my face despite his injuries. This makes me even angrier. I've beaten him, but he still wants to kill me.

"Stop it!" I scream in his face.

He doesn't respond or slow down his attacks.

"You've lost! You can't hurt me; don't you realize that?"

He spits and continues struggling to break free from my grip.

I apply more pressure, restricting his ability to breathe. "I've won. I could kill you if I wanted to, and you're still trying to hurt me? Is this what you want?"

His face is turning beet red, but his lips turn up in a smile. This *is* what he wants.

Scared, I drop him.

He wasn't expecting it and lands hard on the pavement. A second later, he's back on his feet and attacking me.

I push him back, but he comes at me again.

I push him back harder, knocking him to the ground. It takes him longer to get up, but he still attacks me.

I don't even feel his blows and stop fighting back.

"Come on!" he screams in frustration. "Kill me! You know you want to, so do it!"

"No."

"You're a coward! A coward!"

Tears roll down his cheeks as he takes a few steps back and runs at me again. I step out of the way, and he trips and falls to the ground.

Kyle lies still where he landed before turning over, but he doesn't try to stand.

"Just do it!"

"No."

I shake my head in pity.

"Do you think you're better than me? Is that it? You've killed before, Connor. Don't act like we're different. You just don't have the guts anymore." Kyle looks at his broken hand and winces. He spits out a mouthful of blood. "You probably think I'll *face justice* or some other stupid idea, don't you? I'll let you in on a little secret, Connor. Justice isn't the same for people like me. I'll tell them the magtonium made me do it. I'll tell them it drove me mad and I'm sorry for what I did and they'll eat it up."

"And I'll tell them you're lying."

Kyle cackles hysterically. "Do you think they'll really care about what you say? Do you think they'll take the word of someone wearing a mask over a president's son? I'm practically a prince, Connor. They'll listen to me. Do you know why? Because it's easier. It's easier than trying to convict me in court. It's easier than trying to find a jail to hold me where I'll be safe. They won't risk a war with

Kaldonia over the deaths of a handful of people no one cares about."

I try to ignore him, but my blood is boiling.

"Do you know what the best part is, Connor? After they decide it's not worth punishing me, I won't stop. I'll find a way to hurt you. I know who you are. I know who your friends are. I know who your family is. And I'm patient. I'll take my time. When I hurt them, when I kill them, no one ever will know I did it. No one, that is, except you. You'll know, and I promise you will never forget."

The magtonium shifts around my body and forms a series of interlocking plates. My hand is balled it into a fist and glowing red with unfamiliar energy.

I gaze at Kyle. He's looking at my fist too. His face is pulled tight, and he's squinting.

He's bracing for a hit.

"No," I say.

I turn my back on Kyle and walk away.

He screams again - threats, curses.

But I don't turn back.

FORTY-FIVE

My head is swimming as I walk away. I look down at my hands, but I don't recognize them. In my Omni suit, my hands still felt like they belong to me, but now they feel strange and alien.

I want the magtonium suit to disappear, but I stop myself from willing it to happen. I'm still in the city. The area is deserted for blocks, but it would be hard to explain who I am and why I'm here when I eventually cross a police barricade.

"Omni!" someone calls out, shaking me out of my daze.

Down the street, Halpern is jogging toward me, a phalanx of armed Agency employees following close behind.

"It's you, isn't it?" he asks, giving a cursory examination of my suit.

"Yeah, it's me," I say.

Halpern waves the other employees on. They run in the direction I just came from.

"What the hell happened?" Halpern asks.

"It's over. I stopped him."

"And took his clothes too, I see. Nice touch."

"This wasn't intentional," I explain as I observe the magtonium covering my body.

"Then you wouldn't mind handing it over for us to investigate?"

"I don't think I'm in the best place to make that decision, but I'll think about it."

"You don't have to lie. We both know you won't hand it over to us or anyone else. It was worth a try, though."

I'm not sure if he's right. The idea of these nanites crawling all over my skin and interacting with my biology in ways I don't understand is seriously creeping me out. I can't wait to get out of here and get this stuff off me.

"I'm sorry we couldn't do more to help, but it was too dangerous to send my people in. We didn't mean to leave you hanging, considering the condition your metabands are in."

"The condition my metabands *were* in."

"Yeah, I know. One of our drones got close enough to catch the tail end of your encounter. I heard what Kyle said…"

Oh, crap. Did Halpern hear Kyle use my real name? Does he know who I am?

"Oh, okay," is all I can think to say.

"Unfortunately, he's not wrong."

"Huh?"

"About him facing consequences."

"Oh, that. Right. Of course."

"What did you think I was talking about?"

"No, that's what I thought you were talking about."

Halpern raises an eyebrow, but he appears confused enough that I'm sure he isn't keeping anything from me.

"Anyway," he continues, "we'll do all we can to make

sure he faces justice for his crimes, but we can do little more than deport him back to Kaldonia. Once he's there, he likely won't face any consequences."

It feels like a punch to the gut. Part of me was holding out hope there was *something* someone like Halpern could do to put Kyle behind bars, but even his power has limits.

Halpern must sense my disappointment because he moves to place a hand on my shoulder. I reflexively move back, scared the nanites might harm him. Halpern notices, but he places his hand on my shoulder anyway.

"Don't worry, I'm not scared of this stuff. You've got it under control."

"I don't know that I do."

"I trust you. You've got more willpower than anyone I know. If anyone can keep these little suckers in line, it's you."

"Thanks, but I don't know if you rea—"

"I mean it," he says. "You could have killed Kyle Toslov. He killed just to increase his power, and you would have been well within your rights to end him. I would have let you walk right out of here too. But you didn't. You kept your cool and risked your life by not crossing that line. I'm proud of you, and I'm glad we're on the same side."

"So, does this mean I'm not banned from Agency facilities anymore?"

"A metahuman who goes by the alias Omni is banned from those facilities. As far as I can tell, you're not a metahuman, so who's to say it's the same person underneath that mask?" he says with a smile and a wink. "It'd be helpful if you could come in and talk in the next couple of days for my official report. In the meantime, get out of here. We'll handle the cleanup. You've earned yourself some rest."

FORTY-SIX

A week later, life is getting back to normal. I even got let back into the academy. The moratorium on metahumans is still in place, but Michelle got me back into the school. She didn't mention it, but a couple of days later, Derrick told me they'd broken up.

He promised it was unrelated to anything I did and blamed it on how much they both work. Derrick has never been great at balancing his work as a reporter with his actual life, so I take him at his word.

Jim is still asking me a million questions a day about the magtonium in my possession. I'm not annoyed by it—yet. There's a lot about the nanites I don't understand, and with Midnight still off the grid, it's been great to talk through some of my discoveries with him. I'm still a ways off from trusting the magtonium like I trusted my metabands, but I'm getting there.

Sarah has also been an incredible help. She even apologized for giving me the cold shoulder over the past few months. I told her I completely understood why she was mad at me for not telling her my secret, but after Kyle attacked her, she said she appreciated the need to keep identities a secret. I told her I still wished I'd let her in on my secret earlier, but I'm glad she knows it now.

I'm happy we're back on decent terms again, even if we're just friends. It's good to have another person to bounce ideas off of, especially when that person knows way more about robotics than I could ever dream of learning myself.

Okay, so it's not just robotics. She's smarter when it comes to anything science-based.

Fine, she's smarter than me when it comes to pretty much everything.

She's also been working to repair her mech suit. She says her progress is slower than she'd like, but once Midnight gets back she hopes he'll be able to answer a few questions to speed things up.

A few days after my fight with Judgment, I made a trip up to Iris's hideout. I'm nowhere close to feeling confident enough to fly using the magtonium suit, but luckily, Derrick lent me his car.

That's not entirely accurate. I was able to *take* Derrick's car and return it to the garage before he noticed it was missing. His addiction to work comes in handy sometimes.

As I pulled up to the house, John Armstrong emerged. He told me Iris wasn't there before I could turn the engine off. I asked him a few questions anyway, but he pleaded ignorance. He said he didn't know where she went or how long she would be gone.

As I left, he offered a glimmer of hope.

"Wherever she had to go, she'll be back. She always comes back."

FORTY-SEVEN

I'm sitting in my dorm room, head buried in a math book, desperately studying for a test in Muldowney's class when a text message lights up my phone.

Alleyway between the hospital and apartment building on Worth St. 9pm. Sewer cap.

The text is from an unknown number, but it's obvious it's from Midnight. I pick up the phone to ask where he's been, but I know he won't answer. He's communicating over an insecure channel and won't give more information than necessary.

It's already after 8:00 p.m., so I need to leave now. I consider my options, and then decide I can always study later. The test isn't until next week so I don't need to panic. I'm used to studying the night before anyway.

So this is what being semi-responsible is like, huh?

Without using the magtonium, I'll have to sneak off campus and grab a bus into the city. Luckily, I have at least three different ways to sneak out of this place without getting caught now.

I wave at Jim, who is studying at his desk with his headphones on. He doesn't notice me, so I stand closer to him and try again. Then I notice he's not engrossed in his textbook at all. He's asleep.

Probably best to let him sleep.

I REACH the alleyway at 9:06. With the coast clear, I duck into the alley and search for the sewer cap Midnight mentioned in his text. This is something that would have puzzled the hell out of me when I first met Midnight, but now I can guess the sewer cap is an entryway. I find a sewer cap peeking out from under a dumpster and push the it out of the way.

Nothing about the cap looks out of place or unusual. I place my hand on it, and a soft blue glow emanates to verify my palm print. Once it finishes, the cap slides into a hidden cavity. A ladder stretches into the darkness. The alleyway is dimly lit, making it difficult to see down the opening. The ladder looks standard, nothing technologically advanced about it.

I place my foot on the first rung and lower myself into the hole. After only a few steps, the sewer cap slams shut inches above my head with a loud clank, startling me.

It's pitch black, and I have no way out of here except down. I cautiously lower my foot onto the next rung and continue down until everything around me is illuminated all at once. I discover the ladder continues for another hundred rungs or so.

I readjust my grip and continue. It's a frustratingly slow way to get underground, but I suppose I've been spoiled by the elevators at the academy.

"You're late," Midnight says as my feet touch the ground.

"I didn't factor in the time it'd take to descend the longest ladder I've ever seen in my life. Have you given any thoughts to installing an elevator? Even a fireman's pole would be a huge help."

There's no response.

I'm standing in a cavernous abandoned subway station. It's so large it takes me a couple of seconds to locate him. He's seated and hunched over a workstation in the far corner, and I make my way over.

"Hey. Long time, no see," I say.

"It's been a week."

"Right. Still, that's a while, and you were MIA before that. You're really burning the candle at both ends. Have you ever considered taking a vacation?"

Midnight doesn't respond.

"Would you take the cowl off at the beach, or do you not care about the tan lines?"

He pushes his chair back from the workstation, and I see that he's working on a small sample of magtonium.

"Is that from Kaldonia?" I ask.

"Yes. Do you have your magtonium with you?"

"Yeah," I say. I pull a smooth black metallic ball from my pocket. "I figured out how to get it to configure itself into this little package. Well, Sarah figured it out, but I offered moral support. Pretty cool, huh?"

"I strongly recommend you stop using it."

"Huh? But I just got it, and with my metabands gone, it's all I've got."

"Your metabands aren't gone. They were absorbed into the magtonium with the others."

"Okay, then with my metabands completely disintegrated and being used as fuel, the magtonium is all I have. Are you going to give me any hints about why you're so concerned?"

Midnight pulls his cowl back. I suspect he sleeps in that thing, so I know this is serious.

"The Kaldonians have claimed magtonium is a naturally occurring mineral that exists only within their borders. We knew from the experiments at Wichita Meadows it's anything but natural. It wasn't clear if Kaldonia was lying to protect the secrets of the nanotechnology they had built, but I strongly suspected that wasn't the case. Kaldonia never had the means to produce that type of scientific breakthrough. So the question became, if Kaldonia didn't create magtonium, who did?"

"Let me guess. It was aliens?"

Midnight stares at me.

"Wait, are you serious? I was joking. You can't be serious. Are you seriously being serious?"

"The magtonium was sent to Earth to destroy every metaband on the planet. The intent was to have the magtonium wander the world consuming metabands. If my calculations are correct, the magtonium would have only needed to consume a few metabands before becoming unstoppable. But a corruption in its software prevented it from carrying out its mission. Kyle Toslov took advantage of that bug to overwrite pieces of the operating system and inject his own artificial intelligence to change magtonium's behavior."

"How in the world can you know this?"

"I found the vessel the magtonium came from. It's too massive for the Kaldonians to move, so it's in the same spot where it crash landed, deep within the forests of the Kaldonian countryside. The perimeter isn't well guarded. They're relying on the remoteness of the area to keep the ship a secret. Once I found the location, getting inside was a trivial matter."

"Hold on, I'm still wrapping my head around the fact aliens exist. How are you so calm about it?"

"In the future, it's common knowledge alien races exist."

"Yeah, well, we're in the present, and I'm kinda freaking out. Who are they? What do they want? And why did you say *races*, as in multiple types of aliens? That's not helping me with the whole not freaking out thing."

"This race is unknown to me. The planet they inhabit has only been observed from a distance. It showed no signs of life or any remarkable features. Therefore, it has never been visited. It's possible that in my future the planet was already abandoned or suffered a cataclysmic event that wiped out all life. It's also possible they have cloaking technology to protect them from view."

"If they're not around in your future, how do you know anything about them?"

"The magtonium was sent to our planet as a message, and there's not much use in sending a message if the recipients can't understand it."

"What do you mean?"

"I'll show you."

Midnight rises from his chair and walks over to a wall of computer displays, motioning for me to follow. He taps a few keys on the keyboard. The screens flicker to life, and a video begins to play. The footage is shaky and looks like it's from the perspective of someone walking through a dark hallway.

"Is this the inside of the ship?"

"It's a recording from my cowl's onboard sensors. Just watch."

A ghostly red figure fills the frame. It appears to be a hologram. The figure looks human, though, and it's wearing clothing that wouldn't look too out of place on Earth. The quality of the hologram isn't great, and it's hard to gather many details.

"That's an alien? It looks just like us."

"People of Earth..." the hologram speaks.

"They speak English too!" I shout.

"Connor, please. Just watch," Midnight says.

"The false queen is no more," the hologram continues. "By the time you view this message, the weapon on board this ship will have already begun to neutralize your abominations. This is for our own safety and serves as retribution for the years of cruelty you have inflicted upon our planet. We possess other, more powerful weapons that you could not even imagine in your worst nightmares. Any attempt to retaliate against the people of Volaris will be met with an extreme and overwhelming response. Consider this your first and final warning."

The hologram flickers out and disappears from the screen.

"What... the hell?"

"I don't know what that means either, but we have an even bigger problem. Their warning shot malfunctioned, and they seem to have been made aware."

"How do you know? Is there another message?"

"No, this is the only message I could find. The ship was abandoned otherwise. Its only purpose was to transport the magtonium to Earth. The crash landing must have damaged the ship's onboard systems. That's why the magtonium never carried out its purpose."

"How do you know they're aware it failed? If the ship

was damaged, maybe its communication system was knocked out too?"

"Unfortunately, that isn't the case. It took some doing, but I was able to commandeer and reposition a NASA deep space telescope to find Volaris."

Midnight returns to the keyboard and the screen changes to display a blurry white dot in a sea of blackness.

"Is that Volaris?"

"No, it's something much worse."

"I don't understand. It doesn't look like anything."

"That's because it's still billions of miles away. If I had to guess, based on its size and speed, that tiny white dot is a warship, and it's heading for Earth."

THANK YOU

Thank you so much for taking the time read my book. If you enjoyed it and would like to leave a review I'd really appreciate it. Reviews help out indie authors like me immensely and make sure I'm able to keep putting out more books.

To stay in the loop on all things *Meta*-related and otherwise, please sign up for my mailing list at tomreynolds.com/list. You'll be the first to hear about new releases, sales and other fun stuff. No spam either, I promise.

ALSO BY TOM REYNOLDS

Meta (Meta: Book 1)
The Second Wave (Meta: Book 2)
Rise of The Circle (Meta: Book 3)
Midnight Strikes (A Meta Prequel Story)

ABOUT THE AUTHOR

Tom Reynolds lives in Brooklyn, NY with a dog named Ginger who despite being illiterate proved to be a really great late night writing partner.

You can sign up to hear about new releases by joining his mailing list at tomreynolds.com/list.

- amazon.com/author/tomreynolds
- twitter.com/tomreynolds
- instagram.com/tomreynolds
- facebook.com/sometomreynolds
- bookbub.com/authors/tom-reynolds

Printed in Great Britain
by Amazon